SPOTLIGHT SCANDAL

STELLA BIXBY

FERRY TAIL PUBLISHING LLC

For the Good Kathy. Thank you for helping me launch my author career and for always believing in me. I appreciate you more than I can express.

My part was coming up. My line. My single line.

I couldn't mess it up.

I'd messed it up too many times already.

My scalp tingled in anticipation. My hair was changing. It would probably turn blue and tighten into ringlets.

But I couldn't think about my hair.

I needed to focus on my line.

How did it go again?

I'd stumbled over the words so many times I was getting them all jumbled in my head.

My hands shook at my sides. The lights were so bright.

How could I be this nervous when there was no one in the audience?

What would happen when the theater was full?

I'd be the laughingstock of Cliff Haven.

I'd be driven out of town.

I'd be—

"Ellie?" Katie asked from the front row.

The rest of the cast groaned.

I'd missed it.

Completely missed it.

"Sorry, Katie," I said. "We can try again."

"It's okay," Katie said. "Let's take a break. You've all been working hard this morning."

Katie was the director and practically the queen of our little Iowa town. Stylish in her own eccentric way, she wore zebra-print leggings, tall black boots, and an oversized Christmas poncho that mirrored the stage backdrop. I wouldn't have been surprised if she'd had it made specifically to direct this musical.

"Can you really not remember?" Bex asked, handing me a water bottle. "Or is it nerves?"

"I just get all freaked out," I said. "I think it started with me not remembering but then it transformed into this big ugly beast in my head and now every time I even think about those words I want to throw up." I took a sip of the water. "You know it's only going to be worse when they string me up fifteen feet above the stage."

Bex laughed. She was by far my best friend in town. I'd only moved here a few months before, but she'd instantly given me a job as a waitress at the café and taken me under her wing. "I'm sure Katie would replace you."

"She won't," Melody—a gorgeous blonde in sleek black leggings and an off-the-shoulder silver sweater—said, coming up next to me. "I've already asked her. She has a lot of faith in you. More than she should, if you ask me."

Melody was Katie's daughter and a legit Hollywood actor. She likely didn't mean to come off as rudely as she did. She was simply used to being around the best actors. I couldn't imagine how frustrating it would be dealing with the likes of us . . . the likes of me.

But Katie insisted everyone in town have a fair shot at being in her productions. She'd purchased the theater before Melody was born and had been directing plays and musicals ever since. People from all over came to see Katie's productions.

"She'll get it," Bex said. "She has to work out her stage fright. Any chance you have pointers?"

"Have a drink before the show," Melody said with a laugh. "But seriously? Practice. Write the words on a piece of paper and say them over and over again. You only have one line, but sometimes that makes it more difficult. That line doesn't have to be perfect, but it does have to be said."

Melody checked her phone.

"Expecting a call?" Bex asked.

"My agent should be calling about a role," Melody said. "It's kind of a given, but if I don't get it, it might be an indicator that my fifteen minutes are expiring."

I sighed. I was worried about saying one line while Melody worried about her entire career. If she wasn't able to say one simple line, she'd get fired.

But she also got paid the big bucks to remember her lines. And I'd like to see her deal with a surly old man whose pain had reached a point where he'd actually had to ask for help. I guess we all had our strengths. Hers was acting. Mine was dealing with said surly old men.

"Oh, there she is," Melody said, tapping her phone and pressing it to her ear. "Hello?"

Melody listened for a minute, then said, "Are you sure?"

Bex shot me a questioning glance.

I shrugged. I couldn't tell whether she was happy or not.

"Uh-huh," Melody said. "Uh-huh. Okay. Yeah. Thanks."

She dropped the phone to her side.

"So?" Bex asked. "Did you get it?"

Melody looked at us with tears in her eyes. "I guess my time is up."

"What do you mean your time is up?" Katie said, walking up behind her. "Who was on the phone?"

Melody composed herself, clearing her throat once, then turned to face her mother. "It was my agent. I didn't get the role."

Katie's face flashed anger, then resolve. "Then you'll get the next one."

"They went with someone . . . softer," Melody said, shaking her head. "They said I was in too good of shape."

"Did you tell her I'd feed you all the cookies and cake you wanted?" Katie asked.

Melody didn't answer.

"Come on," Katie said, wrapping an arm around Melody's shoulder. "It'll be okay. So you didn't get the role. We've gone through it before and come out the other side."

Melody nodded once, as if she'd accepted a command from a drill sergeant.

"Now—" Katie turned her attention to me. "—can I talk to you for a minute?"

"Sure," I said.

As Bex and Melody walked away, Bex said, "Suck it up, buttercup."

"I'm really sorry," I said to Katie. "It's not like I don't know the line. I do. It's just—"

"Stage fright," Katie said. She glanced back at Melody, then leaned closer. "Melody had it too. Her first role was a disaster."

"How old was she? Two?" I laughed.

"Three," Katie said. "But she was a baby thespian, and that's exactly what you are right now. You're going to be great. But you will have to say the line."

"I will," I said. "I promise."

"I only wish Esme had been in your life." Katie sighed. "She would have enrolled you in classes here at the theater. Heck, you and Melody might have been fighting for roles in Hollywood right now."

I doubted that. Melody might have had stage fright as a toddler, but she had an incredible amount of natural talent.

"I wish I'd grown up here too," I said.

Esme was my grandmother. I'd never met her—she died before I got the letter she sent me—but she'd left me her farm, which brought me to Cliff Haven. Almost everyone in town loved and missed her.

"Keep practicing," Katie said. "And maybe have a drink before the show." She nudged me and laughed. Like mother, like daughter.

A pang of jealousy coursed through me at the thought. Emily, my mother, had run away. No one even knew she had a baby. She left me at a fire station when I was born, and I'd gone through more foster families than I even wanted to count.

If she had known my hair would have been such a problem, would she have kept me? Or found a magical family for me. Was I even born without magical color-changing hair? Sometimes I thought about what it might have done when I was a baby and how my foster families would have reacted.

I chuckled at the thought.

"There's that smile," Katie said. "I didn't know it could exist inside these walls."

"I'm sorry," I said.

"Stop apologizing." Katie sighed. "I know you can do this. It might be hard, but you can do hard things, Ellie Vanderwick. You are one of the strongest people I know. And I know a lot of people."

"Thanks," I said. "You're right. I can do it. I'll keep practicing."

"Good," she said. "Also, I've been meaning to ask—have you seen Bonnie lately?"

Bonnie was an outsider like me. She only moved to town because a bunch of people died, and she was the next in line to inherit a farm and the town hardware store she had absolutely no interest in owning.

Okay, so they hadn't simply died. They were murdered.

Either way, Bonnie used to come to our morning workout groups but had since stopped.

"Sometimes I see her through her kitchen window when I'm getting home at night," I said. "Why?"

"I invited her to be part of the production, but ever since, I feel like she's been avoiding me."

"She could be busy with the store," I said. "I'm sure it's difficult balancing that and the development company."

"That might be it," Katie said. "I thought she and I would be friends."

"If I get the chance, I'll talk to her."

Katie smiled. "Thanks."

"Maybe she heard about the curse," Nancy—one of Katie's friends and a rock-and-roll Mrs. Claus lookalike—said, peeking up from one of the seats a couple of rows back.

"What are you doing back there," Katie chided. "You're supposed to be making lunch."

"Fran and Amy said they could handle it," Nancy said. "And I needed a nap."

"Long night doing nails?" Katie asked, her tone sarcastic.

Nancy owned Nancy's Nails. Cliff Haven also had Katie's Café, Fran's Feed and Fabric, Belinda's B&B, and Amy's Antiques. So basically, women ran the town. The men were mostly farmers.

"What were you saying about a curse?" I asked.

"This place is jinxed, cursed, voodooed," Nancy said, her jolly cheeks reddening with every word. "Every time we put on a production, one of the actresses gets hurt or dies."

"Now, hold on," Katie said. "That's not true. No one got hurt during last summer's play."

"Bex sprained her ankle," Nancy said.

"On the front steps," Katie said. "That's not technically in the theater."

7

"It's on the property," Nancy mumbled.

"And only one person died years ago."

"Even so," Nancy said. "Someone *died*." Her eyes went wide with the last word.

"Who died?" I asked. "How did they die?"

"The trapdoor was faulty," Katie said. "It was a complete accident."

"Unless it wasn't." Nancy wiggled her white eyebrows.

Katie reached out to smack her playfully, but Nancy ducked out of the way with a giggle.

"Don't listen to her," Katie said. "She's full of stories."

"It's not a story," Nancy sing-songed as she hurried to the doors that led to the lobby. "By the way, lunch is ready."

My scalp warmed. I pulled my ponytail over my shoulder to see my hair transition to a light blonde.

"That's pretty," Katie said.

"If only I could keep it this way," I said. "It would go well with my costume."

Most of the people of Cliff Haven were used to my semi-magical hair. Esme and Emily—my grandmother and mother—had the same hair. It wasn't unusual that I let my hair do its own thing when we weren't expecting visitors in town.

My entire life, I'd done everything I could to hide my hair. It was the only thing keeping me from staying in one place for more than a few months. It had ruined every relationship I'd ever had, cost me jobs, and almost got me kicked out of college.

Before I came to Cliff Haven, I only had Penelope and Mona. Penelope was my mini pet pig, and Mona was our traveling home—a Volkswagen Microbus. After I graduated college, we traveled all over the country but ended up returning to Colorado before getting the letter from my grandmother.

"Should we get some lunch?" I asked Katie.

"You go ahead," Katie said. "I need to check on Melody."

"She'll be okay, right?" I asked. "It's not like this could really end her career."

"An actor is only as relevant as their next job," Katie said. "If there is no next job . . ." She shrugged and walked away.

If one good thing came out of me being left at a fire station, it was that I never became an actor. Especially when I couldn't say one silly little line.

2

W e didn't end up going through the play a second time, after all. Melody refused to return, and she was the lead.

When I got home, I had plenty of time to change and get ready for a session I had scheduled with Amy. She had troubles with her lower back from moving all the large antiques around her shop. We'd been working through the kinks.

With the town's help, we had renovated the barn behind my house into a fitness and healing studio. A big metal sign over the doors had shown up overnight without a peep as to who made it. It said Relief with Ellie —the same name I'd painted on the side of Mona for the times I traveled to clients. Not everyone wanted or had the ability to come to my studio. I loved working with older adults. Having a way to meet their needs in their own homes was something I absolutely had to be able to do.

Amy walked through the doors two minutes before

her session. Her hair was dyed neon green. She wore gray sweatpants and a hoodie with some heavy metal band on the front. It was likely she had on a t-shirt of the same sort underneath. Where Katie was eccentric, Nancy was jolly, and Fran was tough, Amy was my punk-rock granny.

"How are you today?" I asked.

By the way she was walking, I could tell it would be a rough session. "Not great," she said, her voice raspy from being a smoker most of her life. "I tweaked my back, and the chiropractor said there was only so much he could do."

"Can you tell me where it hurts?"

She took off her sweatshirt to reveal exactly what I expected—an oversized t-shirt with a metal band on the front.

"Right here," she pointed, and I took a couple of notes.

Amy didn't like to be touched, which made it more challenging when she needed to deepen her stretches. Usually, if a client allowed for it, I'd assist them in the stretch, but I never wanted to breach the client's boundaries. In fact, I didn't want to get anywhere near their boundaries.

I was a person who valued my own boundaries. I knew how much it hurt when someone didn't respect them.

"Let's start with a few gentle stretches," I said, demonstrating what I wanted her to do.

We'd been working through various pains in her back for weeks, so she could likely do these independently, but if I let her do it independently, I'd have no business.

"Ooh, right there," she said. "That feels fantastic."

"Here," I said. "Take the back of this chair and try to deepen the stretch, as long as it doesn't increase in pain."

She did, but the look on her face was that of struggle.

"Fran told me Nancy brought up Renard's Curse this morning," she said.

Amy and Fran lived together. The town didn't talk much about their relationship—nor did they—but it didn't matter to me one way or the other.

"Renard's Curse?"

She grumbled a bit and tried to deepen her stretch by pulling on the back of the chair. "The one at the theater," she said. "Katie won't admit it, but it strikes every time she puts on a production."

"And people get hurt?" I motioned for her to change direction with the stretch.

"Women get hurt. A woman even died once," she said. "I guess it's a good thing we have a witch in town to help us solve the murder."

"No one is going to die." I laughed. "And I'm not a—"

"Witch. Uh-huh, sure." She paused. "How's it going with Melody?"

I was a bit caught off-guard with this question. "Fine," I said, not sure if I was supposed to say anything about the rejection she'd gotten. "Katie seems thrilled to have her here for the play."

"I don't mean with Katie. I mean with you."

"With me?" I asked.

"Don't play dumb," she said. "I know there's a small rivalry there. That's another thing the theater does. Brings out rivalries. There was even one between Esme and another woman way back when. And now you and Melody."

I had a hard time believing Esme had a rivalry with anyone. In my mind, she was a total saint. I almost asked about it, but Esme's friends were tight-lipped when talking about her. I couldn't figure out why, but eventually they'd come out with it.

"Let's go back to the stretch that felt the best," I said, not wanting to talk about Melody and me. It wasn't like she and I were mean to one another. I guess there was a bit of jealousy on my part. Before she came to town, Katie and Earl—Melody's father—had taken me under their wings. Katie even gave me Melody's old clothes. But since Melody returned, their focus has been more on Melody. And rightfully so.

"Do you feel like you can go deeper in the stretch?"

Amy struggled against the chair. "Oh, for heaven's sake," she said. "Why don't you just help me."

I could feel it in her words that she wasn't sure.

"Are you certain?" I asked. "Because I can find another—"

"Do it," Amy said, closing her eyes.

I put one hand on her shoulder and the other on her hip, telling her everything I was going to do before I did. Then I helped her deepen into the stretch.

"Breathe," I said. "In and out, and when you let the breath out, stretch a little deeper. If it hurts more than a stretch, tell me right away."

She took a breath and finally seemed to relax.

We held the stretch for a few more deep breaths.

"I can't quite remember, but I think Emily had a rivalry too," Amy said between breaths.

"Really?" I asked. I tried not to sound too eager for information. "With who?"

"I-I don't know," Amy said, her eyes closed. "The memory is foggy. But I think it was a relative. An older relative." She shook her head as if trying to dislodge the idea.

"If it was a relative, that would mean they would be my relative too." I could feel excited little sparks coming from my scalp. "Was it a woman or man?"

"A girl," she said. "They were young."

I released her from the stretch.

She opened her eyes, a teary gloss covering them. "I'm sorry I can't remember more. It's weird. Fran keeps telling me to get my mind checked, but I remind her we're no spring chickens. We're getting old."

"How's your pain?" I asked. "Do you feel any better?"

"I think so."

Sometimes she had more movement or said she didn't feel as bad. But she never said she felt better.

We moved through a few more stretches, not talking much.

I was lost in thought about Emily's relative.

As we were wrapping up the session, I gave her a few tips about drinking water and continuing to stretch every day.

I glanced at the calendar on my phone. "I have you on the schedule a week from now. Does that still work for you?"

In response, she wrapped me in an enormous hug. I froze for a minute, not sure how to react.

I patted her on the back, and she slowly let me go. "I can't believe how much better I feel," she said. "Thank you so much."

It was times like these I loved my job.

3

A fter Amy left, I used the time to practice my line in the studio when no one was there to watch.

I turned on calming music and took some deep breaths. The barn studio was one of my many happy places. Looking around made me smile. If I couldn't say this line here, I wouldn't be able to say it anywhere.

In my nicest handwriting, I wrote the line on the mirror. All I had to do was repeat it.

But did I write it correctly?

I checked the photo of the script on my phone to make sure.

Yep. It was right.

Deep breaths. I needed to say it. Say the line over and over again. Once I had the line down, I could add in the acting.

Ha!

The acting. As if I'd be able to act out this silly little line.

It was so simple, so why was it so hard?

The words were there. I just had to say—

"Anyone in here?" Bonnie peeked her head in the door. She wore black leggings and what looked like an expensive chic winter jacket and matching faux fur-lined boots.

"Yeah," I said. "Practicing for the play."

"Ah, the play," Bonnie said.

"Katie said she invited you?"

"She did," Bonnie said but didn't explain any further.

"Are you doing okay?"

"That's why I'm here," she said. "I saw Amy leave and thought I could sneak in to see you before your next client. I'll pay you, of course."

"The rest of my day is clear," I said. "What sort of pain do you have?"

"I don't know if it's pain, per se," Bonnie said. "But my lower back is so tight. I think it's from all the reaching and squatting and lifting and twisting I do at the hardware store."

"Let's see where you're at." I ran her through a variety of stretch tests so we could gauge her progress. "We might not be able to fix all of this in one session."

"I hear you have magic hands," Bonnie said.

"Magic hair, maybe. Hands? I'm not sure."

"So your hair is magic?" Bonnie's eyes widened.

"If you call changing at a moment's notice magic, then sure." I laughed. "Let's start with some stretches. Do you mind if I help you into the stretches, or would you prefer I don't touch you?"

Bonnie smiled. "I don't mind."

17

As she moved into the first stretch, I helped with a hand on her shoulder. "How does that feel?"

"Fine."

"Tell me if anything hurts."

"Everything hurts," Bonnie said, her voice changing.

"Then let's stop."

"No, not like that," Bonnie said. "The stretch is fine. It's my heart."

A wave of grief washed over me. "I'm so sorry." I didn't know what else to say. I wasn't sure whether the grief I was feeling was my empathy for her situation or Bonnie's actual grief radiating from her body through my hand and into my chest.

"Since PJ and Percy died, I've been so lonely," Bonnie said. "They were my world. Everyone thinks I was the bad guy, but I knew nothing about Helen or this town. I thought Percy was busy traveling."

The same way Helen had.

I'd been the one to find Percy lying dead in my cornfield. I hadn't known then how his death would rock the community.

"Now, I live in the house where PJ was murdered. And you know what's weird? I feel like if I leave, I'm leaving him there." I couldn't see her face, but her body heaved with a sob. "But I don't want such a big house."

I was about ninety percent certain she didn't want advice—just someone to listen.

"Helen's Hardware has an apartment on the second floor. I could easily live there. But what about PJ? Would leaving mean I was giving up on him? Forgetting him?"

"No," I said before I could stop myself.

She straightened up and looked me straight in the eye. I couldn't read her emotions until she wrapped her arms around my neck.

I hugged her back for at least a solid minute before she let go.

"Thank you," she said. "For listening. And it seems your magic fingers did the trick."

I laughed. "I'm so sorry about PJ and Percy. You always seem so strong that I think people forget you're grieving too."

"You know, I made lots of excuses in my head about why I didn't want to do the play—the biggest being running two businesses."

That seemed like a legitimate reason not to take something else on.

"But in reality, I guess I didn't want to be vulnerable in front of the entire town." She looked down at her perfectly manicured nails. "And that's what acting is—being vulnerable. Putting yourself out there for everyone to judge. Do you think that's why you're struggling with your lines?"

"How did you—"

She glanced at the words I'd written on the mirror.

"My first time on stage, I froze like a winter pond in Canada."

"Wait, your first time?"

She looked down at the floor. "I went to school for the arts—the performing arts." She shook her head. "But I haven't been on stage since before I had PJ."

"Well, I know Katie would love to have you."

"I'll think about it." Bonnie looked up at me. "I better get going."

"Drink lots of water and keep stretching."

She reached inside her purse and handed me a hundred-dollar bill. "I don't have anything smaller, but I don't need change."

I gaped at her.

"Unless it's more, then I have—" she rummaged in her purse again.

"No," I said, stopping her. "That's plenty. I helped you stretch for ten minutes. You don't even need to pay me."

She looked up at me. "Never tell a paying client not to pay you," she said. "You're in business. The only way to stay in business is to make money."

She would know, she not only ran the hardware store, but she also ran a multi-state development company.

"Uh—right—then thanks," I said. "I'm glad you stopped by."

She smiled. "Better. Now, get back to practicing."

I glanced at the mirror, and dread settled in my stomach. I would never get it right.

When Bonnie opened the barn door, Penelope came trotting inside.

"If it isn't my sweet little piglet," I said, scooping her up in my arms. "How was your day?"

She oinked and wiggled her nose against my cheek.

"That's good," I said. "I'm not getting anywhere with this line. Let's go inside and have some dinner."

When I started toward the door, Penelope wiggled and squealed—her way of telling me to let her down.

And the moment I did, she charged to the back of the barn.

I sighed and followed.

Usually, when she did that, she needed to show me something.

At the back of the barn was a magical mural my mother painted.

I'd hung a heavy curtain across the width of the barn, separating the mural from the studio and giving me a place to meditate and appreciate my mother's work. It made me feel close to her, somehow. And it almost always surprised me with its changes.

Today was no different.

Typically, the mural showed the barn and the house. Sometimes it showed only part of the barn or house, but the farm was always the setting. It was the people and animals that changed.

With the barn as the backdrop, a woman in the painting sat cross-legged with her back to me. Her white hair flowed down her back, nearly touching the ground.

My hair had been long before, but never that long.

Next to her sat a man. It was hard to tell from the back, but if I had to guess, the painting was of Emily and Jake.

Jake was the police officer—or rather police chief—who arrived on scene when I found Percy's body. With one glance at his blue eyes, I thought he could have easily been my father. When I found out he and Emily had been an item, I thought it was a sure thing. But he refuted the possibility, saying he and Emily had never taken their relationship to that level of intimacy.

They might not have made love in the physical sense, but from the look of the two of them in the mural—hands interlaced, bodies leaning toward one another—they were obviously in love. From what I could tell, Jake still hadn't gotten over her. He assured me he'd do everything to find her if she was out there.

But I wasn't confident. If she left, she must have had a reason. And that reason was probably enough to keep her from ever coming back.

4

I'd tried to practice the words again after I finished studying the mural, but my stomach was growling. And after dinner, Penelope and I barely made it to bed before falling asleep.

When I showed up to rehearsal the next day, the theater was silent. I checked my phone. Had I messed up the schedule? I was certain we were supposed to have morning rehearsal. My calendar confirmed it.

But where was everyone? Usually, the auditorium doors were open, and people meandered around talking about the latest town gossip.

I carefully opened one of the doors, trying not to make too much noise. On stage, a beautiful woman with bright orange hair recited Melody's lines. If I hadn't heard Melody's version, I would have been convinced this woman was made for the role. She had to have been from Hollywood too. Maybe a friend of Melody's?

I tiptoed through the door and down the aisle to slide down in the seat next to Bex.

The entire cast was in the seats watching this woman perfect Melody's lines.

"Who is she?" I asked so quietly, I wasn't sure the words had actually come out of my mouth.

"Trinity Lawson," Bex whispered back. "Melody's rival from the next town over—Poppy Hills."

"She's phenomenal," I said. "Why is she saying Melody's lines?"

"She's auditioning for understudy." Bex shifted in her seat. "She's the last one. There were four or five others this morning."

"That's great," Katie said, standing from the front row. Trinity smiled.

"If you could head back to the dressing room with the others, we'll be in shortly to announce our decision." Katie sat back down and leaned over to talk to Melody.

The rest of the cast took this as their chance to stand and stretch.

"I didn't realize I was supposed to be here early," I said.

"You weren't," Bex said. "I'd only gotten here a few minutes before you."

Katie stood and turned to us. "Thank you for your patience," she said. "If you'd like to take a quick bathroom break or get some muffins Amy and Fran made this morning, please do so. We'll begin rehearsal in ten minutes."

An angry-looking Melody stood and followed Katie onto the stage and back into the dressing room. I'd be angry too if someone could say my lines as well as me.

The thought made me smile. Literally anyone could

say my lines as well as me. Mainly because they'd actually be able to say the lines.

"Let's get a muffin," Bex said. "Katie's been trying to get Amy and Fran to bake for the café, but they refuse."

I could understand why she'd want their muffins. They were sweet with tangy blueberries and granulated sugar on top. I ate two before a group of women came out of the dressing room. Four of them looked upset. Trinity—the one with orange hair—looked thrilled.

She spoke excitedly to another of the women who had tears streaking down her face.

Katie and Melody walked into the lobby behind them —Melody looking like she'd taken a bite of an especially tart lemon. But her face shifted from disgust to surprise in a split second.

When I turned to see why, Trinity jumped into the arms of an exceptionally handsome man. He wrapped his arms around her waist and lifted her off the ground as she squealed, "I got the role."

Everyone in the lobby turned to look at Katie and Melody.

Melody's face turned bright red. "What she means to say is she got the understudy role."

But Trinity didn't seem to care that it was an under-study role as she planted a huge kiss on Hot Guy's lips.

"That's Dylan Bram," Bex said, leaning into me. "He's Melody's ex-boyfriend."

"From Poppy Hills?"

"No, he went to school here," Bex said. "But appar-ently, he has no sense of loyalty." She said the last word so loud, a few people turned to look. Bex shrugged and pushed her braided black hair over her shoulder.

"It's okay," Melody said, coming to stand next to us. "She's always wanted what I had. I guess she doesn't mind being sloppy seconds." Melody took a deep breath. "He and I are ancient history, anyway." I thought I might have seen a tear in her eye, but she quickly blinked it away.

"I'm sure if you're not up to practice today, you could skip it," I said.

"You obviously have no idea how all of this works," Melody snapped. "If I skip rehearsal, she'll step in for me. And if she steps in for me and does a better job? Then she'll step into my role."

"I'm sure Katie wouldn't give her your part."

Melody raised her eyebrows. "Are you?"

I thought about all I knew of Katie. She was kind but tough and wasn't one to pull punches. "Maybe?"

"Mom does what's best for the production. Always has. She gave my role to my understudy my junior year of high school because I thought my boyfriend was more important than rehearsal." Melody looked over at Trinity and Dylan. "I'll give you two guesses who she gave my role to."

"Trinity?" I asked. "And Dylan was your boyfriend at the time?"

Melody nodded. "I guess you can't have it all."

"I thought you were dating that hot celebrity," Bex said. "You know, the one from that new action movie."

Melody teared up again—for certain this time. "He broke up with me last night."

"Last night?" I asked. "Why?"

"Our relationship was more of a business deal than anything else." She cleared her throat. "The minute I lost that role, he could contractually move on."

"Contractually?" I asked. "You had a contract with your boyfriend?"

"I don't expect you to understand anything about show business," Melody said.

"I may not understand show business, but I understand emotion," I said. "And it looks to me like you actually liked him. In more than a business deal way. Like if you had color-changing hair, it would be a shade of deep blue right now."

Bex laughed. "Wouldn't it be funny if everyone's hair changed depending on their moods?"

"With a wig or some dye, anyone's hair can change," Melody said. "You thought that's Trinity's natural hair color?"

I shrugged. "I hadn't really thought about it."

"Wasn't she blonde in high school?" Bex asked.

"Blonde and brunette, but apparently, she had to go orange for this one." She rolled her eyes. "Come on, let's get on with rehearsal."

"Is this where I'm supposed to be?" Bonnie said, coming up to stand next to us. "What's going on?"

"It's a long story," Bex said. "Melody's high school rival got the understudy role. She's hugging Melody's high school sweetheart. And Melody got dumped and rejected for a role yesterday."

Bonnie grimaced. "That's rough."

"It's okay," Melody said. "The show must go on, as they say."

"Okay, okay, that's enough," Katie said, her pretty purple cape flowed behind her like a curtain in a light breeze. "I think it's time you left, Mr. Bram. We're about to start rehearsal."

He kissed Trinity one more time before lowering her to the ground.

Melody averted her gaze.

"That's quite enough," Katie said, her tone harsh. She may have been judicious when we were on stage, but Melody was still her daughter. She would not let Dylan and Trinity parade around, trampling her little girl's feelings.

Rehearsal was full of fits and starts. My line was the very last of the play, and we didn't made it even halfway there. Which was fine by me.

But the reason we didn't was wrapped in a pretty package named Trinity—the girl who had the face of a porcelain doll but acted like a complete and total diva. If I didn't know better, I'd think she was the Hollywood star and Melody was the hometown sweetheart.

Every time Melody said a line, Trinity made a comment. Whether it was to Katie, Melody, or herself, everything Melody did came under scrutiny.

Until Katie had enough.

"I think we need to call it a day," she said. "Melody and Trinity, can I please see the two of you in my office?"

I sighed and walked down the stairs off the side of the stage.

"That practice was pointless," Bex said, meeting me in the lobby. "Other than those scrumptious muffins. I think I'm going to grab one more."

"You go ahead," I said. "I need to talk to Bonnie for a second."

Bonnie hadn't been able to participate much. There wasn't exactly a role for her since we'd started practicing a couple of weeks before. But she seemed happy to be there.

"Hey, thanks for coming," I said as Bonnie took a bite of the triangle sandwiches Nancy had prepared for lunch.

She finished chewing and swallowed before saying. "I had a really pleasant time. Thank you for inviting me."

"Do you think you'll come back?"

"You know, I didn't think I'd have a place in the production. Especially since it's been cast and all. But I think I will." She smiled conspiratorially.

"Is that right?" What was she suddenly so interested in?

Bonnie and I turned to watch Melody stomping through the lobby and out the front door.

"Yes," Bonnie said. "I'll see you later." She turned and followed Melody outside.

Bex returned with two muffins in her hands. "I'm heading to the café to check on the Charlies," Bex said. "Wanna come with and get some crispy-edged pancakes?"

I loved their crispy edges of pancakes. "That sounds awesome." I pulled my hair out of the bun and let it drape over my shoulders. It was back to its normal white after probably being about a million different colors on stage.

As we were walking out the doors, Melody and Bonnie were deep in conversation.

"Can you believe she'd ask Mom to cast one of her friends too?" Melody said. "After being so awful up there all day?"

Bonnie leaned in and whispered something that made Melody's eyes widen. "Do you think that would work?"

Bonnie shrugged. "It did when I was on stage."

"Please tell me you're not plotting something terrible," I said as we walked by.

They both smiled at me. "Just talking theater tricks," Bonnie said.

Melody laughed.

Katie probably wouldn't love Bonnie and Melody bonding, but it was sweet that Bonnie seemed to be taking Melody under her wing.

"Be careful," I said. "The last thing we need is someone to prove the curse is real."

"Wait," Bonnie said. "What curse?"

I glanced at Melody. "Why don't you tell her."

Melody nodded and started into the explanation.

"Now, let's get those pancakes," I said, hooking my arm into Bex's and starting off toward the café.

5

Snow was starting to fall when we walked into Katie's Café. Bex and I both worked there, though Bex was the manager, while I filled in when needed.

When I'd first arrived in Cliff Haven, Bex had taken a chance on me and given me a job. Now that my therapeutic recreation business had taken off, I mostly visited for the pancakes.

"Did you hear Trinity Lawson is in town?" Big Charley asked when Bex and I walked back to the kitchen.

"She's Melody's understudy in the play," I said, pulling off my hat.

"She's staying at Belinda's B&B," Big Charley said.

"That's strange," Bex said. "Why wouldn't she stay in Poppy Hills? It's only a few miles away."

Big Charley shrugged. "Maybe because of the snowstorm coming? You should have seen all the luggage she had. You'd think she was moving in." He looked around to make sure no one heard what he was about to say.

"Belinda told me she thinks something's going on with her. Very suspicious."

"How so?" Bex asked.

Big Charley shrugged. "I guess she didn't want to give Belinda her whole name—even though Belinda knew exactly who she was—and rented two different rooms."

"Ooh," Bex said. "That is strange."

"She probably got the other room for Dylan," I said.

"As in Dylan Bram?" Big Charley said.

"They're dating," Bex said. "But I would guess if he's staying there, he's staying in her room." She wiggled her eyebrows for effect.

I laughed. "But isn't Dylan from around here? Couldn't he stay with his parents?"

"His parents moved to Florida the minute he graduated high school," Big Charley said. "It was too cold here for them."

"I feel terrible for Melody," I said. "First, the role. Then being dumped. Now this? I guess it's true—when it rains, it pours."

Big Charley shrugged. "All I know is Trinity better be careful. Melody's not a girl you want to mess with."

"Melody's harmless," Bex said. "I know you still think she's the one who killed your cat, but she wasn't. That cat was on its last leg when it bit her. It probably had a heart attack when she screamed."

"You don't know," Big Charley said, his eyes filling with tears. "You weren't there. And Fluffy was my best friend."

"That was almost twenty years ago," Bex said. "It's time to move on, buddy." She patted him on the arm.

"Pancakes are done," Little Charley said, handing me a plate of steamy deliciousness.

"Aww, thanks," I said with a smile.

Little Charley blushed. Not only was little Charley—well—littler than Big Charlie, he was also a fraction of Big Charley's age—probably in his early twenties. If I'd have grown up in Cliff Haven, he likely would have been a couple of grades younger than me.

I took my pancakes to the dining room and sat in the staff booth toward the back near the local table where the farmers gathered in the morning to drink their coffee and tell their stories. Currently, the table was empty, as was most of the restaurant.

Bex tied her waitress apron around her waist and leaned against the wall next to me. "Do you think there's really something suspicious about Trinity?"

"No," I said. "I think certain people like to make gossip where there is none."

"I have no idea what you're talking about," Bex said with a laugh.

I took a bite. "It should be illegal to make pancakes this good."

Bex rolled her eyes. "I don't know how you don't get fat eating all these pancakes."

"Um," I said. "I have a recreation business. I work out all the time."

"Stretching can't possibly burn that many calories," Bex said.

The bell on the door dinged, and Bex glanced up. When her eyes widened, I peeked around to see who had walked in. It was none other than Trinity, though her hair looked like she'd run a brush through it the wrong way.

"It looks like she got into a tussle," I said. "You don't think Melody beat her up or something, do you?"

Bex dipped her chin and gave me an are-you-stupid look.

"What? Do you see her hair?" I asked.

"Maybe she teased it up." Bex shrugged. "I'll see what I can find out."

Bex went to take Trinity's order.

I tried to listen, but they were too far away. Instead, I pulled out my phone and checked the latest news. The winter storm and blizzard warnings were the first news in my feed, but when I scrolled down, my heart sped in my chest.

I glanced up where Bex was still talking to Trinity. The same Trinity whose face my thumb hovered over. The same Trinity who had apparently landed Melody's role.

"Why do you look like you got punched in the gut?" Bex asked, walking back over to me.

I turned my phone so she could see the headline:

Small-Town Rival Beats Out Hollywood Royalty

"Oh no," Bex said.

"Do you think Melody knows?"

"That could be why Trinity kept her sunglasses on and her head down the entire time."

I gasped. "You think Melody beat her up?"

"She didn't seem to have much of an appetite," Bex said. "She only ordered egg whites and dry toast."

"What if that's what Bonnie told Melody to do?" My scalp tingled at the thought.

"Bonnie did not tell Melody to beat anyone up," Bex said. "This is not middle school."

I thought back to how brutal girls were in middle school and shuddered. "Thank goodness for that."

Bex nodded in agreement.

"You probably shouldn't tell Big Charley about this. Or that she's here," I said, glancing toward the kitchen. "Especially if she wants her space."

"Good point," Bex said.

I finished the last bite of my pancakes and left a twenty on the table. "Thanks for the cakes. I should probably go home and practice my line."

"It's one line," Bex said. "How hard can it be?"

I tried to laugh, but my voice caught in my throat.

"I'm kidding," she said. "It is a pretty important line."

"Yeah," I said. "See you later."

I snuck a glance over at Trinity as I walked out the door. She still had her head down—her messed up orange hair draped over her face.

Penelope was sitting at the door of the barn when I pulled into the driveway. The snow was falling harder now and had covered part of her back and her head.

"What are you doing out in the cold?" I asked, rushing

over. She had a door that led to the house, but not one into the barn. I'd never seen a need, and since I tried to keep the studio as clean as possible, I didn't really want muddy little piggy prints all over it.

I brushed off the snow, scooped her up in my arms, and she nuzzled my nose with hers, like usual.

"Do you want to go in the barn again?" I asked.

She oinked loudly.

"I'll take that as a yes."

When I opened the door and set her down, she charged back to the mural like she had before. I flipped on the lights and followed.

"What is it this time?"

The painting had changed.

Today, there were two people again, but one was different. They were both women. One had white hair and could have been Emily or me based on the age. Or—I suppose—Esme when she was much younger. She was turned away like normal.

Not a single person had ever been facing me.

Until now.

The other woman stared—or I should say, glared—straight at me. I'd never seen her in the mural, but she looked somewhat similar to Trinity. At least the Trinity with the teased hair. She wore big sunglasses, had a crooked nose, and high cheekbones. Perhaps this was a rendering of Trinity before she had some sort of plastic surgery? Or maybe it was a different woman with the same hair?

A glint in her eye seemed to be more than a speck of paint. It seemed real. Like a tiny speck of magic had wafted in on the breeze and imbedded itself in the painting.

I reached up to touch the speck, and when my finger came in contact with it, a zap of electricity wound its way around my knuckles, spiraled up my arm, climbed the length of my neck, and made my hair feel like it had been roasted over an open flame.

I yanked my finger away to find the speck gone. When I pulled a strand of hair in front of me, it was burnt orange.

Just like the woman's in the painting.

Just like Trinity's.

Penelope and I ate our dinner and headed to bed early, but I couldn't sleep. The memory of the electricity coming from the mural kept replaying in my mind. And no matter what I did, I couldn't get rid of the orange hair. It was like the magic had changed my hair permanently. Which, in a way, would have been nice if it wasn't for the color. I wasn't particularly fond of orange.

But if it stayed the same color, at least I'd be able to dye it or cut it without it simply growing back or changing back within minutes of my doing so. When I was a particularly hormonal teenager, I'd tried to shave my head. Within an hour, my hair had all grown back. I hadn't tried to shave it again.

I snuck out of bed, careful not to wake Penelope, and tiptoed down the stairs to the front door. I wrapped a magical jacket I'd gotten from Xander—a warlock friend of mine—around me and shoved my feet into my snow boots before walking outside.

The air was cold—bitter cold—but the jacket made it feel like I was inside. At least the top half of me.

The snow had stopped falling, and the sky had cleared, letting all the heat in the earth escape into the heavens. But I needed my time with Mona. I needed my time with the fresh air and the stars and my breath. When I turned the key in the ignition, Mona barely rumbled to life. But it was enough to get her out of the garage and under the stars.

Iowa wasn't like Colorado. It didn't have as many clear sky days, but when it did, the stars looked like miniature spotlights beaming down from the heavens. I turned Mona off and climbed up to the yoga platform on her roof. Besides the skylight, the yoga platform was my favorite of Mona's features.

I removed my boots, but left my jacket on, then started my yoga flow with deep breaths, easing into poses and keeping my thoughts close. I'd parked Mona, so I wasn't facing the barn. That way, my mind wouldn't go back to what I'd seen—felt—from the mural.

If Emily had painted it, did she have something to do with its magic? Had she embedded magic into the paint? Or had it come from something else? Someone else?

I shook my head gently back and forth as I eased my way back into downward dog. My hair—still orange—fell over the headband I'd put on to keep my ears warm.

I kept moving, stretching, breathing until my brain settled, and I finally felt a bit of peace. As I completed my practice, lying in corpse pose, the stars seemed to sparkle just for me. My breaths came out like little puffs of smoke. Tonight was wrong. All of it. The feeling inside me wouldn't quit.

It was then that an idea popped into my head.

I needed to talk to Trinity.

Immediately.

6

I almost talked myself out of going five or six times in the short drive from my farm to Belinda's B&B. Sure, my hair had changed to be like Trinity's, but that didn't mean I needed to talk to her. It was probably a fluke—a coincidence.

But deep down, I knew it was more than that. I could feel it.

When I pulled up to the B&B, a single light was on inside.

A young woman sat at the front desk giggling loudly at something Dylan Bram had said. He was leaning on the counter, carefully flexing his bicep and smiling at her as if she was the only person in the world.

"Wow, you work fast," I said.

"I'm sorry?" The woman said.

"Not you," I said. "Him."

"I don't believe we've met," Dylan said, turning his heartthrob eyes on me. "I'm Dylan Bram."

"I'm Ellie Vanderwick," I said. "I'm here to see Trinity—uh—"

"Lawson?" Dylan said.

"That's the one," I said. "Unless you're dating two different Trinities. Then I guess I need the one with orange hair."

"Like yours?" Dylan said. "I suppose imitation is the sincerest form of flattery or whatever."

"I didn't exactly choose the color." I inspected a strand of hair that had fallen out of my hat.

"Bad dye job?" Dylan asked.

"Magic," the woman—whose name I didn't even know—said from behind the counter. "She's Esme's granddaughter."

Dylan turned to look at me. "Makes sense."

"Do you know where I can find Trinity?"

"She went back to the theater to run some lines," the woman said.

"Thanks," I said. "And don't let him fool you. He's a pretty big jerk. He dated Melody back in the day."

This stopped his laughter. "What does it matter to you who I talk to?"

I didn't even justify this with a response.

I pulled my jacket tight around me before heading back out into the cold.

Snow covered the sidewalks and streets, crunching under my boots. The news forecasted several inches to fall over the course of the week leading up to the play.

I crossed the road to the theater and reached for the door handle. It opened easily when I pulled, but the inside of the theater was dark. If Trinity was here, she'd have to have night vision. Or a flashlight.

After feeling around on the wall, I finally found a switch. A single bulb flickered on near the hallway leading back to the dressing rooms, but it was enough light to see where I was going. I wasn't one to be terribly jumpy, but all the talk about the curse of the theater didn't exactly give me the warm and fuzzies.

Plus, big buildings in the dark are freaky.

I tiptoed toward the doors leading to the auditorium and tried to peek inside, but the windows were slits and had been covered from the inside with paper to keep people from peeking in.

Beyond the door, it sounded like someone was practicing one of the more boisterous parts of the play—the part when Melody's character argues with Bex's character. It was relatively funny when they did it, but the way Trinity was acting made it sound like an actual argument.

Then my hair tingled. I pulled a strand down to find it was still orange, but the feeling I had told me something was wrong. That and my hair was starting to frizz.

I tried to open the door, but it was locked.

Every door to the auditorium was locked.

The dressing room had stage access. I took off in that direction.

When I turned a corner and ran into total darkness, I was thankful I'd been around the theater for a few weeks, so I knew the layout.

Until I hit a brick wall.

Or what felt like a brick wall?

In reality, it was a person. A very sturdy person

because any average person would have toppled over backward if I'd hit them at the same speed.

"Ouch," I said.

A hand clapped over my mouth, and an arm wrap around my chest.

I tried to yell, but my voice came out as little more than a muffled plea. I clawed at the arm around me, but it was covered in what felt like a thick leather jacket.

"Shhhh, quiet," I heard a man's voice in my ear.

"Let go of me," I said, but with a hand over my mouth, it was unintelligible.

"If you promise to be quiet, I'll let you go."

I recognized the voice and instantly relaxed.

"Good," Xander said. "You can't scream, okay?"

I nodded.

He eased his hand off my mouth and dropped his arm from around me.

I didn't scream.

Didn't say anything.

Instead, I took off running down the hall again.

"Hey," he whisper-yelled.

I could hear his footsteps coming after me, but I knew I was faster than him. I'd beaten him in a race once.

I reached the door of the dressing room and yanked it open.

The light switch was exactly where I expected it to be. I flipped it on to find the dressing room destroyed.

I hurtled over toppled chairs and shattered mirrors. My focus was on the stage. I needed to get to the stage.

What I would do when I got there was beyond me, but

if I didn't get there fast, something terrible would happen. The curse was going to strike again.

I ripped open the door to the stage to find two women. One held her arms in front of her face in a defensive stance while the other kept yelling, "It was mine. It should have been mine."

"Whoa, is the orange hair convention in town?" Xander asked.

Did I mention they both had the same orange hair that had magically plopped itself on my head? One had to be Trinity, but I couldn't be sure which one. They were both tall and slender—one with her arms up and the other with her back toward me.

"Should we step in?" I asked.

"Let me get a better look first." Xander walked away toward the back of the stage. I had to stop myself from staring. I always had a thing for bad boys—the ones who would inevitably break my heart—and Xander in his leather jacket and tight-fitting jeans was the embodiment of the bad boy.

I turned back to see the woman with her arms over her face sobbing as the other kept yelling about something that was supposed to be hers.

A sound came from where I assumed Xander was standing.

"What was that?" The yeller asked.

She stormed off toward the back of the stage to investigate while the sobbing woman sank to her knees and dropped her face into her hands.

"Are you okay?" I started toward her, but a crack came from the stage.

The woman's head snapped up to look at me. "Help, me!" she cried, her face so swollen and covered in bruises and blood I couldn't figure out if she was Trinity or not.

I started toward her, but before I got there, she fell through the floor.

7

Within milliseconds, Xander was holding me by the shoulders, preventing me from running onto the stage. "It might not be stable," he whispered in my ear.

"It's okay," I said. "Let go."

He finally did.

I stepped gingerly toward the opening, but when I got closer, I realized the stage hadn't cracked or broken. It looked like a perfectly cut square had simply been removed.

"What in the world?" I asked.

"It's a trapdoor," Xander replied, running a hand through his shoulder-length black hair. "She fell below the stage."

I peeked over the edge to find at least a ten-foot drop. The woman laid in an unnatural position at the bottom.

"Are you okay?" I yelled down.

"Shhh," Xander said.

I glanced around. He had a point. Where was the woman who had been screaming at her?

"Did you see the other woman?" I asked.

Xander shook his head.

"We need to get down there," I said. "She might be okay."

Xander acted as if he was weighing the pros and cons. But I wasn't about to stand there and let her die.

There had to be a way to get under the stage where the trapdoor led.

I hurried to the stairs that led to the catwalk above the stage and searched for a hatch that might have stairs to go below. It wasn't too hard to find, but when I tried to pull on the handle that popped up out of the floor, the door seemed stuck. Almost as if it had been glued shut.

"Xander, help me," I said. "I can't get this door open."

He took the handle. He must have used his magic because it looked as easy as lifting the lid off a margarine container. I'd tried to get him to help me figure out my own magic, but he was against it. He would say, *"It'll happen when the time is right. You can't force it."*

"I'll go down first," he said, bringing me back to the task at hand.

"You don't have to protect me," I said. "I'm perfectly capable of descending into dark, scary places."

He mumbled something under his breath but stepped aside to let me go.

The ladder was covered in things I didn't want to think about. It was unclear how long it had been since anyone had been down there, but it was safe to assume it had been a while.

Dust permeated the air—tiny specs floated around when Xander flipped on a single hanging light.

"This looks hygienic," Xander said, sarcasm seeping through his words.

We stepped over various boxes and other dust-covered items until we reached the spot where the woman had dropped.

If she was alive, she would have quite the recovery with broken bones and the damage to her face. She might have been Trinity, but I couldn't say for sure. And I didn't want to look any harder than I had to.

I reached my fingers down to check for a pulse. I willed it to be there.

It had to be there.

But it wasn't.

I hung my head and felt an enormous hand on my shoulder. "We should probably get out of here."

"What do you mean?" I asked. "We need to call Jake." I pulled out my phone, dialed his number, and pressed send.

"Jake won't be able to make her alive again," Xander said. "And if we don't get out of here, we might be joining her in the morgue."

"What makes you think—"

But my words were cut off by the sound of the trap-door swinging back into place with a snap.

The light from the stage above was snuffed out instantly, leaving the only light source from a single light-bulb near the ladder.

My phone beeped against my ear. I glanced down to

find an error message. I tried to redial, but Xander grabbed my arm and started dragging me toward the ladder.

"We have to get out before we get sealed in here permanently," Xander said.

"Can you use your magic to get us out?" I asked.

"Not if magic is used to shut us in."

A shiver went down my spine.

He thought someone magical was doing this?

I shoved my phone back into my satchel and moved as quickly behind him as I could.

Even if we were sealed down here, they'd come in for rehearsal and would be able to hear us scream. Wouldn't they? Or would magic keep them from hearing that too?

We reached the ladder, and Xander hurried up first. The entire time, I expected the hatch to fall on Xander's head. But he got to the top and held it open so I could climb through.

"Maybe they didn't know we were down there," Xander said. "We need to get out of here."

I pulled my phone back out. "I'm calling Jake. If someone is here, he needs to get them. Especially if they hurt that girl."

"That's fine," Xander said. "Just follow me while you do it."

He led me back through the disaster that was a dressing room and out the back door to the alley behind the theater. The snow was coming down hard when we walked outside. I pulled my jacket tighter around me and waited for Jake to answer the phone.

"Ellie?" Jake said, his voice tired as if I'd woken him. Which I probably had since it was the middle of the night.

"Someone died at the theater," I said, trying to sound like I wasn't out of breath.

"I know."

"You know?" How did he know? "Are you here?"

"Am I where?" Jake asked.

"At the theater?"

"No, I'm in my bed," he said. "Wait, are you at the theater?"

"Yes," I said. "Someone died here."

"I don't think you're going to solve a years-old case in the middle of the night."

Ah, okay. "Someone died here *tonight*," I clarified.

"Tonight?" Jake asked.

"A few minutes ago," I said. "She fell through the trapdoor."

"The trapdoor has been boarded up," Jake said. Though I could hear in his voice, he was starting to take me more seriously.

"She fell through," I said. "We saw it happen. We went down there and checked, and she's dead. Then the trapdoor snapped closed."

"Hold on," Jake said. "Who are we?"

"Xander is with me."

Xander shook his head. But I'd already said it.

"He was at the theater too."

Xander threw his hands up in frustration.

"Get in Mona, and I'll be there as soon as I can," Jake said.

"You might want to call in a team to check out the place," I said. "The person who opened the trapdoor could still be inside."

"Already done," he said.

8

"Jake's on his way. He's calling in additional officers to check out the theater," I said to Xander when I hung up the phone. "Why didn't you want me to tell him you were here?"

Xander stalked ahead of me down the alley. "I know Jake is your friend, but he's still a cop. And who do you think the cops are going to blame for a murder that looks like magic?"

"How does it look like magic?"

"That trapdoor shouldn't have fallen open like that," Xander said. "But that could have been explained by a bunch of things. What couldn't is that it snapped back shut. By itself."

"There might have been some kind of mechanism." I should have looked when I was down there, but I was too worried about actually getting out that I hadn't thought to.

"And if there wasn't?" he asked.

"Then we'll be looking for someone magical too," I said.

"We?" Xander stopped and turned to me with a laugh. "We won't be doing anything. We are going to let the police handle this."

"You can do what you like. You don't have to help, but you have no business telling me what I can and cannot do."

"I'm trying to make sure you don't get hurt." He took a step closer to me, his features softening.

"I won't get hurt," I said. "But thank you for your concern." I couldn't let his gorgeous eyes and suave demeanor change my resolve to help with this case. Something was weird about it, and I didn't think it was magic.

I walked past him, watching the ground. There were no footprints in the snow here, but as we rounded the corner, fresh prints came from a side door. "Look at these," I said. "Whoever left these was here recently."

The footprints were around the same size as my feet, with what looked like a star pattern on the bottom.

"They look like boots of some sort," Xander said. "Come on. Maybe we'll find someone around the front."

But when we made it to the front, the police were already there, as were several townspeople.

Deb—Bex's sister and one of the Cliff Haven police officers—walked toward me. "Tell me what happened," she said.

"I came here looking for Trinity," I said. "Her boyfriend told me she'd be here."

"Do you think she's the one who fell through the floor?" Deb asked.

"I can't be certain," I said. "She looked right at me, but her face was bloody and swollen. But there was another woman who was yelling. Her back was to me, but she had the same hair and stature as Trinity."

"Let's go back," Deb said. "Trinity's boyfriend told you she was here? Who is he, and when did you see him?"

"Dylan Bram," I said. "Melody's ex-boyfriend. His parents moved to Florida, but I think he's staying at the B&B with Trinity. Or he could be staying in her extra room."

Xander put a hand on my shoulder. Along with the spark I felt every time we touched, a sense of calm wash over me.

I took a breath. "Anyway, I saw Dylan at Belinda's talking to the young woman at the front desk. He told me Trinity came to the theater to work on her lines."

Deb finished what she was writing on her notepad, then looked up at me. "Then what happened?"

"I walked over to the theater. The main entrance was unlocked, but everything was dark, and all the lobby doors into the auditorium were locked." I paused to let Deb catch up with her notes. When she nodded, I continued, "I heard what I thought was a woman practicing her lines, but maybe it wasn't. She was very animated—almost yelling. There's a part in the play—"

"Whoa," Deb said, holding up a hand. "Spoiler alert. Don't tell me what happens."

"Sorry." I took a breath. "When I couldn't get through the doors, I went through the dressing room. But it was dark, and as I turned the corner down the hall, I ran right into Xander."

"And what were you doing in the theater?" Deb asked Xander.

"I had some business to attend to," Xander said. "I had permission to be there."

Deb looked like she wanted to ask more questions but instead turned back to me. "Continue."

"I went through the dressing room—which is destroyed, by the way—and out to the stage."

"I followed," Xander said.

"And then we saw the two women on stage," I said. "Their backs were to us, but they both had orange hair like mine."

"That seems unusual," Deb said. "Then what happened?"

"Xander went to get a better look," I said. "But when they heard his footsteps, one of them darted off stage."

"Those weren't my footsteps," Xander said. "I was barely five feet away from you when they heard something on the other side of the stage."

"Now there are at least five people in the theater," Deb said, making notes. "Did you hear them saying anything that you could make out?"

"The one yelling kept saying something was hers. Was supposed to be hers," I said.

"When the one left the stage area, what happened?" Deb asked.

"The remaining woman sank to her knees and dropped her face into her hands," I said. "When I asked if she was okay, she turned to look at me and said, 'Help me.' That was when I saw her face all bloodied and bruised and swollen like she'd been beaten up."

Xander looked down at me. "You're saying her face was like that before she fell?"

"Yes," I said. "She was unrecognizable," I said to Deb. "And then as I took a step onto the stage, I heard a loud crack, and the woman seemed to disappear through the floor."

"Is that when you called Jake?" Deb asked.

"No," I said. "I wanted to see if she was okay, so Xander helped me open the ladder door that goes below the stage, and when we got to her, she didn't have a pulse."

Deb looked at her notes. "So we're looking at one dead and at least two inside?"

I shrugged. "Maybe," I said. "But there were footprints coming from the door on that side of the building." I pointed. "We made sure to walk around them so they'd still be there for you. Well, they'll be there for a little bit." I looked up at the sky. "If the snow keeps falling like this, they'll be covered soon."

Deb closed her notepad and returned it to her pocket. "I'll check it out. Thank you for your help."

She left to join up with the group of officers that looked ready to storm the place.

"I don't suppose you're going to tell me why you were here before me, are you?" I asked Xander.

"No," he said. "But I had nothing to do with that trap-door opening."

He might have been secretive about—well—basically everything, but he'd never lied to me. Not that I was aware of, at least.

"Are you okay?" Xander asked.

"Why?"

"Because you look like you're freezing to death, and your hair hasn't changed a single time tonight."

"One," I said, "it's cold out here. And two, my hair is stuck because I touched a speck of magic in my mother's painting."

Xander stared at me with wide eyes. "What?"

"You know, the mural in the back of the barn? The one that changes?"

He nodded. He was the only other person I'd met who could see the people in the mural. Everyone else only saw the farm scene. I assumed it had something to do with magic, but I couldn't be sure.

"Penelope has insisted I go back there almost every night. Last night a woman with orange hair had entered the mural. She was looking right at me, which was weird because the people have always had their backs to me, but this one glared at me. She had a little sparkle—almost like a speck of glitter—and when I touched it, my hair changed to look like hers."

Xander gaped at me.

"What?" I asked. "Is that not normal?"

"Nothing about you is normal," he mumbled.

I sighed and turned to look behind me where Jake and Katie were walking up. Katie looked like she'd jumped out of bed, put on the first thing she could find, and rushed to the theater. It was the least put-together I'd ever seen her.

"What happened?" Katie asked, panicked.

"It's okay," I said. "The police are taking care of it."

"Did someone really die? Who? Who was it?" Katie's voice was frantic.

"I don't know," I said. "I didn't recognize her."

"But did you see her? Would you have recognized her?"

Jake glanced at her. "Why?" he asked. "Do you think you know who it was?"

"Melody didn't come home tonight," she said. "Do you think it could be Melody? I know she was really stressed about losing the part to Trinity. I could see her coming up here and working on the play. That stupid trapdoor. The construction guys must not have secured it properly."

"It wasn't Melody," I said. "Unless she dyed her hair the same color as mine."

Katie looked at my hair and winced. "No. I don't think she'd do that." Katie turned back toward the theater. "But that was the color of Trinity's hair."

I nodded.

"Was it Trinity?" Katie asked.

"I couldn't tell," I said. "Her face was pretty badly beaten."

Katie frowned. "This is all my fault. I killed that woman."

9

"Why would it be your fault?" Jake asked Katie. "You weren't even here."

"I'm the one who wanted the trapdoor to be fixed, even though I knew it was cursed." Katie looked down at her feet. "And I gave Trinity and Melody a pretty stern warning today about figuring out their places in the production."

"Did Melody know you were fixing the trapdoor?" Jake asked.

"She and Earl are the only ones besides the construction guys." Katie wiped a tear from her cheek. "I wanted it to be a surprise for the audience. I'm going to call Melody again."

She dialed, giving Jake the opening to ask us all the same questions Deb had.

Xander and I told him the same story. By the time we were finished, the team of officers who had gone into the theater had come back out and given the all-clear.

Katie hadn't been able to get through to Melody, but

the reason was clear when the group of us followed Jake through the door and into the dim light of the lobby.

Melody sat in a chair with a police officer standing next to her as if he expected her to run at any moment. "I found her hiding in the office," he said to Jake.

"I was not *hiding*," Melody said. "I was working."

I thought Katie might drop dead of relief as she fell to her knees in front of Melody. "Thank God you're okay."

"What happened?" Melody asked. "These guys won't tell me anything. They busted down the door in mid-scene and expected me to answer a bunch of ridiculous questions."

"Someone died," Katie said, her voice fragile. "They fell through the trapdoor."

Melody's eyes widened.

"Okay, that's enough," Jake said. "I'm sorry, Miss Katie, but I'm going to have to ask you to wait outside so we can speak with Melody alone."

"This is my theater," Katie said. "And anything you need to ask my daughter, you can ask in front of me."

"It's either this or we can arrest her and take her to the station," the officer standing next to Melody said.

"Arrest her? For what?" Katie stood, her voice going from sweet to mama bear in a half-second.

"What he meant to say," Jake said, "was that we need to talk to her about anything she saw. She was here when the woman dropped through the floor. Plus, we need your help opening the trapdoor. The officers inside can't figure out how to get below the stage. I told them to wait before they went to any drastic measures."

Katie's eyes widened. "They wouldn't dare tear up my stage."

"Let's help them open the door while Deb talks to Melody," Jake said.

Katie looked torn until Melody said, "Go help them. I'll be fine. I did nothing wrong."

Jake led Katie, Xander, and me through the now unlocked theater doors and down toward the stage. Several police officers stood around the perimeter of the stage, seemingly unable to determine where the trapdoor was.

"The lever is back here," Katie said, leading us to the back of the stage.

"Please don't touch anything," Jake said. "We want to make sure we can get prints off the lever, assuming the suspect used it to open the door."

Katie nodded.

I looked all around as we headed back through the curtains and dust-covered floors. It was obvious lots of people had walked back here recently–probably the construction guys trying to get the trapdoor to work— because of the various places where the stage floor was free of dust.

"It's right here," Katie said. "Be careful. It's still very touchy."

That would explain the snapping back into place.

I glanced back toward the stage. I could see the exact place where the woman had been kneeling through a small gap in the curtains. The trapdoor hadn't opened by magic. Someone had used the lever to open it. Intentionally.

When I looked at Xander, he had a puzzled expression on his face.

"How did you get below the stage once the trapdoor was open?" Jake asked. "You mentioned something about a ladder?"

"The ladder's been permanently sealed," Katie said. "But there's a staircase right over here." She led us a few steps to the right, where the top of a staircase came into view. In the dark, it would have been another fall hazard.

"This doesn't look very safe, Miss Katie," Jake said.

"Usually, there's a board secured overtop." She looked around. "The construction workers must have left it off. I'll have to talk to them. Someone could get hurt." She blanched at her words. "Someone else."

"You don't have to come down," Jake said to Katie.

"Maybe I can identify her," Katie said.

"I don't think you'll be able to," Xander said. "Her face was pretty mangled."

Katie squared her shoulders. "We'll see." She stomped down the stairs with so much resolve, you'd think she was the seasoned police officer.

Jake, Xander, and I followed.

I was almost to the bottom stair when I looked up. The catwalk suspended high above the stage moved slightly, and I thought for a moment I caught a glimpse of something orange—hair.

"Hey," I said, turning and running back up the stairs. "Someone's up there." I pointed to the catwalk.

An officer came running back through the curtains.

"Up where?" the officer asked.

"On the catwalk," I said. "I don't see it anymore, but it was there."

The officer hurried off toward the stairs that led up. I kept my eyes on where I'd seen the orange hair.

The officer appeared above me and looked down. "I don't see anyone."

I sighed. The dropping adrenaline and my complete exhaustion could have been causing me to imagine things.

"Keep looking," Jake said. "We're going to go below the stage."

I glanced around one last time before going back down the stairs and following Katie to where the body still lay beneath the closed trapdoor.

Jake shined a light on her, and Katie gasped.

"You're right. I don't recognize her," Katie said. "I'm sorry." She hurried past us and back up the stairs.

"How in the world did she get so beat up?" Jake asked. "It doesn't look like she fell on her face." He felt for a pulse but shook his head.

"Her face was like that before she fell. And she had her arms up like she was trying to defend herself against the woman who was yelling at her," I said. "It could have something to do with the dressing room being demolished."

Jake looked up. "It's a good thing Miss Katie hasn't heard about that yet."

From above us, a scream penetrated the air. "What happened in here?" Katie's voice rang out through the auditorium.

"Scratch that," Jake said. "I think she knows now."

I took another glance around us. The trapdoor above

looked solid. "How is it supposed to work?" I asked Jake and Xander.

"During a performance—when needed—the actual door will stay open," Xander said. "See where she fell?"

I glanced at the concrete floor and nodded.

"Normally, there's an elevator or something that will raise and lower a person through the door." He looked around. "I'm guessing Katie hasn't gotten that far yet with the set up."

"But the door snapping shut would take out the lift," I said.

"The door stays open, and a piece of wood is slipped into place from above to make the stage secure," Xander said. "Katie should have talked to the performers about this."

"She wanted it to be a surprise," I said. "There aren't usually many people on stage at once." I tried to think of the play. There were a couple of times it would have made sense to bring Melody up through the trapdoor. "So then after the play, they take the piece of wood out from above, move the lift, and snap the door back in place?"

Xander nodded. "That's what it looks like to me. It's not like any other theater I've been around, but it seems like it would work."

I almost asked how many theaters he'd been around, but Jake interrupted.

"Do you have any feelings about what happened?" he asked.

"I had a feeling I needed to come here," I said. "But I should have acted more quickly so I could have helped that woman." Regret seeped into my chest. "Otherwise, no. I don't have any feelings."

"Look around," Jake said. "And let me know if you get anything."

Esme had helped him with various cases because she got feelings about them. I'd had feelings, but they weren't as strong as Esme's sounded. And I was hesitant to say anything because I wasn't terribly confident in my ability.

The floor still held Xander's and my footprints, but another set of footprints came from where he and I had been. A tiny set.

"You closed the hatch to the ladder, right?" I asked him.

"Yes."

"Because I think someone else has been down here. Someone with tiny feet."

"What is it with all these footprints?" Xander said. "You'd think these people would know how to cover their tracks. Literally."

"We didn't cover ours," I said.

"We did nothing wrong."

"Maybe they didn't either."

Xander shrugged. "Or they were in a hurry." He looked around. "Do you think Melody did this?"

"I don't know her very well, but she doesn't seem like a murderer to me." I stopped when I saw something shiny on the ground. "Jake," I called out, "can you come over here for a second?"

He gave his guys a couple of additional instructions before he came over. "What's up?"

"I think that might be some sort of evidence," I said,

bending down to get a closer look. "There's no dust on it."

"It looks like a charm off a bracelet," Jake said, not touching it. He called one of the other officers over. "Can you please collect this so we can have a look?"

The officer took pictures of the charm next to a triangular number evidence marker and a small ruler before picking it up with gloved hands and dropping it into a plastic bag.

Jake held the bag up, examining the charm. "It looks like a heart," he said, then handed it to me.

I rubbed a thumb over the small metal heart, and even through the bag, I could feel the magic. My gaze shot up to Xander.

"What?" he asked, his voice alarmed.

"Feel this," I said.

He took it from me and felt the little metal heart. "I don't feel anything."

He handed it back. I felt it again. The hum was still there. "It's definitely magical," I said. "When I touch it, even through the plastic, it's like it's humming or vibrating or something."

"We'll have the lab examine it," Jake said, holding out a hand.

But I didn't want to let it go. Something in me wanted to hold on to this little piece of metal forever.

"Give him the bag, El," Xander said.

I reluctantly handed it back to him. "I know this is a weird request, but if you don't find anything, can I have it?"

"You want a piece of metal from the basement of a

cursed theater?" Xander asked. "Sounds like a bad idea to me."

"I'll see what I can do," Jake said, turning the bag over in his hand for a closer look. "If you find anything else, let me know."

I felt like a tiny piece of me had been ripped out and placed in that bag.

10

Xander and I looked for more clues but found nothing.

When we reemerged from below the stage, Katie and Melody sat whispering in the front row of the auditorium.

"Did you find anything?" Katie asked when she saw Xander and me.

"Not really," I said. I didn't want to talk too much about the case without Jake's approval.

"I hope they can figure out who that girl was and whether this was an accident," Katie said.

"It wasn't an accident," Deb said, coming up behind us. "The trapdoor is securely in place. The lever works as intended, even if it is a bit snappy when the door closes. Whoever you hired to fix it did a good job."

Katie shrugged. "This feels an awful lot like—"

"I've heard," Deb said, interrupting her. "But we can't make any assumptions."

"A lot like what?" I asked.

Katie looked at Deb as if asking permission, but Deb shook her head. "We don't need to spread rumors, especially when there's no evidence proving any connection."

Katie nodded.

"Does it have to do with the other person who died here?" I asked. "The one who fell through the trapdoor?"

Katie's eyes widened.

Deb shook her head again.

Xander looked just as interested as I was.

"We can't discuss previous cases in relation to current cases when we have practically zero facts," Deb said.

"About either one," Katie said.

Deb shot her a glare.

"What?" Katie asked. "The last time this happened, the police couldn't find a single shred of evidence to figure out what happened. It nearly sunk the theater. I don't even want to think about what this will do to the Christmas production."

"I assure you," Jake said, coming through the curtains to the front of the stage. "The show will go on. We'll process the crime scene in time for your dress rehearsals."

"We could rehearse in the barn studio while we wait," I said.

Katie smiled. "Thank you. I'll get the word out." She stood. "But first, you need to go home and get some rest. You look awful."

I didn't know how I looked, but I know how I felt. I needed sleep. "Rehearsal at noon?"

"We'll be there," Katie said.

Xander and I walked outside together to a crowd of people that looked like it might have been the entire town.

"What happened?" Nancy asked, her red coat zipped all the way up over her chin.

"I probably shouldn't say," I said. "I'm sure it'll all come out soon."

As if on my cue, paramedics pushed a stretcher with a black body bag on top through the front doors.

The crowd gasped at the sight.

"Someone died?" Nancy said. "Who?"

"Katie and Melody are okay," I said. "We don't know who it is."

"The curse struck again, didn't it?" Nancy said.

I shrugged. "I don't know. I'm heading home to get some sleep. We'll have rehearsal at my place today at noon."

Nancy nodded and gave me a small hug. "Get some rest. You look horrible."

Xander snickered beside me. "They don't give you much slack, do they?"

"They mean well," I said. "I'll see you later?"

"Okay."

We rarely made actual plans, but I knew deep down that he'd be there for me at the drop of a hat.

I glanced around in the crowd to find all the faces I knew from town. Dylan stood between two women—the one he'd been flirting with at the B&B and a tall brunette I'd never seen in town before. He and the young woman from the B&B stood so close together their arms were touching while he and the brunette held hands, and she laid her head on his shoulder. The thought of him using women like he did made me want to punch him.

I sucked in a breath and turned the key.

It wasn't my problem.

Before heading to bed, I needed to see the mural. My hair still hadn't changed, and I was starting to worry. Not that I needed another thing to worry about.

Penelope was probably still tucked into bed since it was only just around the time we would normally wake up. Still, I had to be quick because once that little piggy's eyes opened, she'd need to go to the bathroom immediately, and I didn't want her trying to take the stairs on her own.

The barn greeted me like a warm hug. I closed the door tight so as not to let the blustery cold inside.

I sucked in a deep breath before pulling back the curtain. The mural looked much like it did before, only this time, the woman with the orange hair faced away from me next to the woman with white hair. And I didn't know if I was seeing things or not, but it looked like a strand of blonde hair poked out from beneath the orange.

My hair was still covered under my hat, so I let it loose, hoping it would help what I was about to do.

There was no sparkle of magic this time when I reached up to touch the mural. When my finger contacted the paint, nothing happened. I lifted it and tried again, but still nothing. It was as if the woman had shut me out by turning around.

I sighed and let my hand drop to my side. Why couldn't I be stuck with pretty pink hair or a nice blonde?

"Are you in here?" Xander said behind me. "I think you need to lea—"

Xander stopped talking when I spun around.

"I need to leave?" I asked. "Why?"

Xander looked like he'd seen a ghost.

"Oh, hey," he said. "I thought you were going to bed?"

"I wanted to see if I could get my hair to change back," I said. "But if you thought I was in bed, who did you think I was?"

"An intruder," Xander said. "I saw someone sneaking into your barn when I drove by, so I wanted to check it out."

There was more to the story, but I probably wouldn't get it out of him. "Do you know why my hair won't change?"

"You said you touched a speck of magic on the paint, and it changed, right?" He glanced up at the mural. "But she was looking at you before?"

I nodded.

"If magic changed your hair, there has to be a reason."

"That's what I thought," I said. "And I'm afraid I missed my opportunity to set things right."

"What do you mean?"

"I should have gone straight to the theater. I could have saved that woman."

"You think the painting was trying to get you to save her?" Xander looked up at it.

"I don't know why else it would've changed my hair this color."

Xander looked at me, then at my hair. "It's a unique color."

"It's hideous." I laughed. Then a thought crossed my mind. "If it wasn't a warning to help save that woman—" I paused. What I was about to say would leave me vulnerable, and saying it aloud was risky.

"Then what?" Xander asked.

If I couldn't trust Xander, who could I trust? "Maybe it was a message from my mom. Like what if she's communicating to me through the painting?"

"I wouldn't get your hopes up about that. But perhaps," he added the last part when he saw the disappointment on my face.

"So magic works on its own accord?" I asked.

"Not usually," Xander said. "It's rare that magic appears without someone—a witch or warlock—around."

"Does that mean there was a witch or warlock in my barn?"

"I would suspect so," Xander said. "The question is, who? And why would they leave some on the painting?"

"It could be a joke," I said, hopeful that it was something simple.

Xander looked at me like that was the stupidest idea I'd ever had.

"Fine, not a joke," I said. "I don't think we're going to figure it out standing here. I'm exhausted, and I'm sure Penelope needs me to bring her downstairs so she can do her business."

"Were you planning on making coffee?" Xander asked.

I wasn't, but the way he asked made me want to. Whether it was pure hospitality or the fact that deep down I wanted him to stay, I wasn't sure. I was too tired to explore my feelings at the moment.

"Sure," I said. "Let's go inside."

We hurried the few steps between the barn and the back door of the house, shaking off the cold and snow when we got inside.

"This storm isn't playing around," Xander said. "I'd be surprised if we would have had the Christmas play even without the investigation."

"Don't say that," I said, hurrying down the hall to find Penelope at the top of the stairs spinning impatient circles. I hurried up to get her. She was fine going up the stairs, but going back down was hard on her little piggy legs. "Katie will be so upset if the show is canceled."

"Someone died," Xander said. "The stage is faulty. And we're all going to be snowed in within hours."

"All of us?" I asked. Xander hadn't ever told me where he was staying.

He shrugged. "The entire state is getting the storm. Roads are closed. The airports are shut down."

I put Penelope down by the piggy door. She ran out into the snow, unfazed by the cold.

"Now," Xander said. "Let's see what we can do about changing your hair."

"How about I put on the coffee first?"

The coffee pot still had the bit of extra coffee in the bottom from the day before. I washed it out, then started making a fresh pot. "How exactly do you think you're going to change my hair? Are you going to use magic?"

"Not exactly," he said. "Don't hate me for this."

I heard him rustling in a drawer in the island.

"Don't break anything. It's not worth it," I said. "Maybe there's nothing wrong with my hair. Maybe it's a glitch." I closed the lid on top of the coffee maker and pressed the brew button.

"Glitches in magic are rare," he said, walking to the other side of the island. "That's not what this is."

"If it's not a glitch, what is it?" I leaned against the counter and crossed my arms over my chest. I was so tired. I could probably fall asleep standing up.

He pulled a knife from a drawer and examined it. "This will do."

"Do for what? Last I knew, coffee didn't need to be cut." I yawned.

"Forgive me," he said, then he threw the knife right at me.

"Xander!" I screamed and fell to the floor.

11

I could hear Xander's footsteps coming around the island toward me. "Still nothing," he said as if it was no big deal he'd thrown a knife at my head.

I peeked up to see him extend a hand to me.

I didn't move. How was I supposed to trust him now?

"Come on, it wasn't going to hit you," he said. "Look." He pointed at the knife as it hovered in the air, inches from where my nose had been mere seconds before.

"You-you're doing that?"

He nodded and plucked the knife from the air, holding it firmly in his grip. "You will be able to do it at some point too."

Whether I laughed because I thought that was funny or because I was breaking into hysterics was beyond me, but I was laughing nonetheless. I took Xander's outstretched hand.

"What did that mural do to you?" He asked, hooking a strand of my hair with his finger. When he touched it, it looked like it started to change color, but he let it drop before I could be certain.

"How did you do that?"

"Do what?" Xander asked.

"Change my hair," I said. "When you touched it, it started to change."

"No," he said. "It didn't."

He took a step back.

"You're willing to throw a knife at my head, but you aren't willing to touch my hair?"

Xander stood in my sweet farmhouse kitchen looking out of place in his biker gear. "I'm sorry, El," he said. "I can't."

I took a step toward him. "Please?" My voice sounded like a whiny teenager's, but I didn't care. "I hate orange. And I feel like this hair is a reminder that I messed up. That I didn't pick up on a feeling—a clue—that I should have."

"I don't think it was a clue," Xander said. "But if it was and someone is planting magic to warn you about a murder, they're probably not the safest person to be around."

The thought sent a wave of panic through me. A murderer might have been in my barn planting magic to tell me they were going to kill someone. A magical murderer.

But it didn't line up. The trapdoor had been released in a non-magical way. At least it could have been. I suppose it could have been released magically as well.

"Either way," I said. "I want my hair back to its normal craziness."

Xander laughed. "Or what? You're going to try to shave it again?"

I laughed too. I didn't remember telling him that story, but it would make sense that I had. "Please," I asked, taking another step toward him. I was within arm's length now.

My hands were shaking, but I reached out and took his hand in both of mine.

His gaze darted from our hands to my eyes. "It won't work."

"Can you try?" I asked with a smile. "Pretty please?"

He sighed. "I'll try."

He lifted his hand out of mine and pulled a strand off my shoulder. Instantly, it changed to white.

"You're doing it," I said, excitement welling in my chest.

I glanced at the hair on my other shoulder, but it was still orange. I picked it up. "Here, do it on this side too."

He obliged, and when his fingers wrapped in my hair, those strands changed too.

Electricity flowed through the ends of my hair to my scalp. It felt soothing. Almost like a weight had been lifted.

"Thank you," I said.

He lowered my hair back to my shoulders and dropped his hands to his sides.

I didn't have to look to know the effect hadn't lasted. The weight was back.

"I was afraid that would happen," he said.

"Why won't it stay?"

Xander wouldn't meet my eye. His focus was on my

hair. He sucked in a breath and said, "I have one more idea. But you have to bear with me."

The heaviness was taking its toll. My eyes were drooping. Exhaustion was taking over. The coffee maker beeped, but I didn't move to pour us coffee.

"I'm up for whatever," I said. "But please don't throw another knife at my head."

He took a step closer, his gaze jumping from my hair to my eyes to my lips and back again. "What I'm going to do is much, much worse." His voice was deep—not in a threatening way—in a way I hadn't heard it before.

I gulped. "What are you going to do?"

He stepped even closer. Our noses were inches from each other.

We'd never been this close before, besides a couple of awkward side hugs.

"Xander?"

He slipped a hand to my lower back. "This is just to change your hair. If you want me to stop, say the word."

What word? Stop? Or word? Not that I wanted him to. He smelled so good. Like espresso beans and sandalwood. How did he smell so good after being up all night? I was certain I didn't smell that good.

"I'm going to kiss you now," he said, bringing me back to what was happening in front of me.

I squeaked out, "Okay," before his lips brushed mine.

Our first touch had sent a volt of electricity through my body, but our first kiss was like lightning hitting a transformer—sparks everywhere. He was right. If my hair didn't change for this, it wouldn't change for anything.

My arms lifted of their own accord, my fingers raking themselves through his hair.

He drew me closer, our bodies touching, his muscular arms wrapped solidly around me.

It might have lasted longer if not for the piercing squeal at the door.

We pulled away from each other like teenagers caught by the police.

Penelope was running figure eights around Xander's ankles, nipping at him like a herding dog.

"Whoa, whoa, stop," he said. "We were getting her hair back to normal. See? It's white again."

I pulled a strand around to the front so I could see. It wasn't exactly white. It was more like shimmering snow when the sun catches it and makes it sparkle like little diamonds. But it didn't change back, even after he stopped touching me. Stopped kissing me.

"Think you can call off your attack pig?" Xander laughed, bringing me back to the situation at hand. Normally, Penelope adored Xander, but apparently, she didn't want us kissing.

"That's enough, Penelope," I said, reaching down to grab her. But she darted away and started running circles around the house.

Xander laughed again, but when our gazes met, it was as if a cloud of doubt washed over his face. "I—uh—I need to go," he said, glancing at his watch. "I forgot there's somewhere I need to be."

"Oh, okay," I said. "Is everything okay?"

"Fine," he said, distracted. "I just—I have—it's nothing." He reached for the handle to the back door.

"Okay, then," I said.

He sighed and walked back over to me, pulled me into a side hug. "I had fun changing your hair." He smirked down at me, but I could tell his usual charm wasn't coming as naturally.

"I did too," I said, hoping for some stupid reason he'd do it again. Kiss me, that is, not change my hair.

But he didn't.

"See you later," he said with one last glance back as he walked out the door.

When he was out, I locked the door and scooped a much calmer Penelope into my arms.

"You silly piggy," I said. "Why don't you want me kissing Xander? You've never had a problem with me kissing men before."

I could have sworn her gaze flickered to my hair before she nuzzled into me.

"You know, if you hadn't been outside playing in the snow, you could have stopped the kiss before it happened." I pulled her closer. "Though, I'm glad you didn't."

She squealed at me, almost as if she was yelling at me.

I laughed. "It was just a kiss." I returned her to the floor. "It wasn't like he wanted to kiss me. He was trying to change my hair back. Heck, he didn't even want to touch my hair at all. But that's probably the way his magic works. Like, it's more potent through an act of intimacy."

The thought made me shiver.

I looked down at Penelope. "It was a kiss with a totally platonic purpose."

I nodded in finality. I wouldn't harp on it. It was a one-time-only kiss.

"I need to go to bed," I said, heading toward the stairs. "Try to stay out of trouble."

Penelope oinked and spun in a circle.

When I was two stairs up, a knock came from the front door.

I couldn't help the smile that came over my face.

He came back.

"Be right there," I said, hurrying back down to open the door. "I thought you had to go—oh."

Xander wasn't the one on the other side of the door.

It was a woman who barely made it up to my chin.

A woman with orange hair.

"**A**re you going to stand there staring at me, or are you going to let me in?" Her voice was monotone and matter-of-fact. Her hair was an exact match to the women on stage, but she was too short to be either of them.

"Who are you?"

"Harriet Nightingale." She shoved a hand out for me to shake. When our palms touched, a spark felt like it went from my hand through the ends of my hair.

Before I could even try to cover it or calm it, I knew my hair changed. Harriet's gaze flitted to the strand hanging over my shoulder and then back to my eyes with indifference.

I pulled the strand in front of me, afraid it would be orange again, but it was a shade of purple. I sighed in relief. "Why are you here?"

"I'm here to solve a murder," she said, pushing her glasses up on her crooked nose. "May I come in?"

"What murder?" I asked. "The one at the theater?"

She ignored my question. "Time is wasting," Harriet said. "Do let me in."

"You're going to have to give me more information before I let you into my house." I stood straighter, towering over her. This woman had a crooked nose like the woman in the mural. She could have been the one who trespassed in my barn and embedded the magic into the paint. "For all I know, you killed the woman at the theater."

"I did no such thing," Harriet said.

"But you were there."

"Perhaps I was," she said. "And perhaps I was not."

"Okay, it's been fun," I said. "But you need to leave now." I started to close the door.

"It is a lovely house," Harriet said. "I recall visiting when I was a child."

I opened the door back up. "You've been here before?"

"Yes," she said, no inflection in her words. "Our grandmothers were quite the pair of what one might call frenemies."

"Is that so?" My pulse raced at the thought of her knowing Esme.

"Your grandmother was a wonderful woman," she said. "I recall her making delicious hot chocolate with homemade marshmallows."

"What else do you remember?"

"I am quite cold outside," Harriet said. "Won't you please let me in?"

It could have been a trap. She could make up a story about Esme, and I wouldn't have known the difference.

But my hair wasn't giving me any indication this woman was dangerous.

"Would you like a cup of coffee?" I asked, remembering the pot I'd put on for Xander. I laughed to myself. How dumb was I to think Xander was at the door? Like he was going to come back and kiss me again? Was this some sort of chick flick where he realized how much he loved me and couldn't stand to be away from me any lo—

"Coffee sounds fine," Harriet said.

I cleared my throat and stepped out of the way so she could come inside.

"Tell me more about Esme," I said as we made our way to the kitchen.

I poured Harriet a cup.

"Do you take any cream or sugar?"

"Black is fine," she said. "And about Esme—I was so young, I don't remember much. We ice skated on the pond, drank hot cocoa, and stayed in Dewdrop. My grandmother—Veronique Nightingale—and Esme loved playing card games, though Esme won most of the time."

I loved hearing stories about Esme and Emily.

"What about my mother—Emily—did you know her too?"

"That's why I'm here," Harriet said.

"You said you're here to investigate a murder," I said, realization hitting me. "Are you saying Emily was . . ."

I couldn't even say the last word. I didn't want to think about it. I was still hoping Emily was out there somewhere. That someday I'd get to meet her.

Harriet sipped her coffee, then stared at me with her piercing blue eyes. "I don't know about Emily, but my mother—Ambeline Nightingale—was murdered. And I believe the night she was murdered, she and Emily were together."

I gasped. "Do you think Emily had something to do with your mother's death?"

Harriet didn't answer right away. "It might seem that way."

Penelope let out a low oink, notifying me of my changing hair, but it was unnecessary. I was aware of what was happening. If she thought my mother killed hers, she could be dangerous. My hair was likely shifting from blue to red.

"But no," Harriet finally said. "I think whoever killed my mother may have had something to do with Emily's disappearance."

"How would you know that?"

"Because of this." Harriet held out a broken silver bracelet and a couple of charms that had come off. "I found it below the stage at the theater tonight."

"So you *were* there," I said, glancing at her tiny feet. "Those were your footprints under the stage, weren't they?"

She didn't reply but held out her hand so I could examine the pieces that looked exactly like the piece I'd found. The piece I'd wanted to keep.

"How do you know it was my mother's?"

She held it out further for me to take.

"I'll show you," she said, dropping the pieces into my upturned palm.

The minute the metal hit my skin, I felt the same warmth I had when I touched the heart through the bag, only the feeling was intensified without the plastic barrier. It was as if a heated blanket covered my entire body. In that instant, I knew it was my mother's. There was no question.

But when Harriet pulled out a picture, it confirmed it. In the photo, a woman with orange hair like Harriet's had an arm around the woman I so desperately wanted to know. A woman who had my hair, my cheekbones, my lips.

And she was wearing the bracelet.

"When was this taken?" I asked.

Harriet set the photo on the island countertop and took another sip of her coffee. "I believe it was taken a couple of months after you were born."

This settled into my stomach like a heavy stone. "But she looks so happy."

"Why wouldn't she be happy?" Harriet asked.

I wasn't about to discuss my feelings with a woman I barely knew. But if Emily was that happy after she'd turned me over to someone else, she likely hadn't wanted me after all.

"Do you know where this was taken?" I picked up the photo, hoping to get a feeling from it, but it simply felt like a cold piece of paper in my hands.

"If you look in the background, I think you'll figure it out," Harriet said.

I looked more closely to find what looked like the seats in the theater auditorium.

"My mother died that same day," Harriet said. "The official police report says it was because of a trapdoor malfunction. That idiot Jake Mulroney thought he'd try to pull the wool over everyone's eyes, but I knew it wasn't right."

"Wait, you think Jake covered something up?" I'd never known Jake to be anything but honest and fair.

"I don't know that he did on purpose," she said. "But it was his first investigation. He was trying to prove himself. And in doing so, he concluded that a faulty trapdoor was responsible for my mother's murder when in reality it was a total setup."

"A setup for what?"

She took another sip of her coffee. "You look tired," she said. "Are you sure you want to go over this right now?"

I was tired. But I was also intrigued. And I knew if I tried to sleep, I'd be unable to calm my thoughts.

"I'm okay," I said.

Harriet shrugged. "There's an old family feud. As you might have guessed, I am a witch too. Though, from what I hear, I have far greater control over my magic than you over yours."

I could feel the blush rising in my cheeks. "I don't consider myself a witch."

"Whether you consider yourself one is neither here nor there," Harriet said matter-of-factly. "The feud started many years ago and is still present to this day. That is why someone also tried to kill me last night."

I stared at her. "What do you mean someone tried to kill you last night?"

"At the theater," Harriet said. "I was lured there under false pretenses. Someone said they had information about my mother's death. I should have known better. It's too bad those other women were there. Wrong place, wrong time, I guess." She shrugged as if it didn't matter that someone had been killed in her place.

"Let me get this straight," I said, taking a breath. "You came to town to find out about your mother's death from many years ago. You went to the theater last night to get information from an unknown person. And when they thought you were on the stage, they opened the trapdoor, killing that innocent woman?"

I might have been tired, but that made absolutely no sense. "Not to be rude, but you're tiny. That woman was at least six foot in her heels. How in the world did anyone mix the two of you up?"

"Did you not notice the hair?" Harriet said.

"But there were two of them," I said. "How could the murderer have been sure one of them was you?"

"I believe he saw the stage after the other woman heard the creak and walked to the back."

"Did you know these women?"

"I didn't," Harriet said. "They were fighting—one beating the senses out of the other—when I arrived. I tried to tell them to leave. That their lives were in danger. Especially wearing those ridiculous wigs."

"Wigs?" My head was spinning.

"I guess they were convincing enough," Harriet said. "If they would have simply left, they might still be alive."

"I assume one of them is," I said. "Maybe we should talk to her."

"Good luck," Harriet said. "If I had to bet, that girl is probably a thousand miles away at this point."

"You were on the catwalk when I was walking down the stairs, weren't you?"

"Perhaps."

I had so many questions. My mind was racing. But I was also exhausted.

"I wish I could stay up and talk more, but I think I need to get some sleep," I said. "You're welcome to stay if you'd like." She may have been a stranger, but something inside me knew she wasn't dangerous.

"I too had a long night and could use some rest," she said. "Is Dewdrop still here?"

She was referencing one of the rooms upstairs. Each room had its own name and personality. And from what I could tell, they chose their guests. If you weren't meant to be in one of the rooms, it would lock you out or make the bed so uncomfortable you wouldn't be able to sleep.

"I'm not sure if it's the same as when you visited, but yes, it's still here," I said. "Would you like to rest there?"

Her face widened into a small smile. "I'd like that very much."

As we headed upstairs, Penelope carefully following behind us, Harriet said, "When we wake up, can we take a spin on the pond? I haven't been ice skating in ages."

I laughed. "I'm sorry to tell you, but the pond is no longer there." I'd been all over the property. It was large, but once the corn had been harvested, I wanted to make sure I knew the lay of the land. And in that exploration, I'd never found a pond.

"It's not out there past the grove of trees?"

"There are no trees other than the ones surrounding the house. It's all farmland."

Harriet didn't dispute this, but I could tell she didn't quite believe it either.

"That's too bad. I have a lot of memories from that pond," she said. "Esme was the best skater. She twirled like an angel. Then she'd help me with my spins." She looked back at me. "It's too bad you never met her."

I could feel my hair changing. Probably a jealous green.

"Did Esme leave a recipe book of any kind?" Harriet asked, continuing up the stairs.

"Not that I've found." There was only one book Esme left—a temperamental journal that only allowed me to read its words when it wanted me to.

"It's nice to be back in a house that has magic."

The word magic made me stop in my tracks.

"A house that has magic?" I asked. I mean, I knew the rooms were slightly magical in their deciding who stayed and who went, but other than that, the house seemed perfectly normal to me.

"Sure," she said. "Can't you feel it? You do have Esme's gift, do you not?"

"I'm not sure I know what you're talking about." I was sure, but I didn't want to give anything away she didn't already know. Plus, it irked me she knew more about my family and my life and even me than I did.

"The hair thing. The healing. The feelings. You have it."

I definitely had the hair thing. The healing? It was possible. It did seem like a lot of my clients recovered rather quickly from their ailments after I saw them. The feelings, though? Not as much. I mean, I'd had feelings, but I wasn't very good at figuring them out yet. Hence the reason a woman was now dead. I winced and tried to bite back the guilt threatening to take over.

"I have some of it," I said. "Since you know so much about my—er—magic." I still hadn't come to terms with the fact that I was magical. "Why don't you tell me about yours?"

"Perhaps after we sleep." She turned the knob to Dewdrop, and the door swung open easily for her. "Looks like it remembers me."

A thought popped into my mind. "Did you mess with my mother's mural?"

"Your mother has a mural?" She looked genuinely confused. Apparently, that was a no.

"I'll see you in a while," I said. "I have rehearsal at

noon in the barn. If you want to come down, feel free. Otherwise, there's food in the fridge. You can help yourself."

Harriet nodded. "And after your rehearsal, we're going to solve this murder."

"Which murder?" I asked.

She shrugged. "Both, I suppose."

"After rehearsal, we can talk about it."

"I know you probably don't want to get in the middle of this," Harriet said. "But whoever murdered my mother might be in town looking to kill again."

Fear rushed through me. If that person was in town killing people and looking for Harriet, what would stop them from finding her in my house?

"You didn't leave any indication you'd be coming here, did you?" I asked.

"Do I look stupid?" Harriet asked. "I've been looking for my mother's killer for years. Ever since I turned sixteen and my grandmother could no longer keep me under lock and key."

"Sixteen?" I asked.

"Do you not know anything about magic?"

"I grew up in foster homes," I said, anger welling up inside me. "Unlike you, my mother didn't tell anyone she was pregnant with me."

"She told one person," Harriet said.

"Who?"

"My mother."

"Well, a lot of good that did anyone, huh?" I threw my hands in the air, and Penelope oinked beside me. "If I had grown up with my mother or grandmother as I should

93

have, I'd know more about magic. I'd know about whatever you're talking about. But I didn't. Your grandmother might have kept an eye on you until you were sixteen, but when I was sixteen, I was living alone in a van."

"The same one in your garage?" Harriet asked.

"Let's talk about it later." I began walking toward my room—the master bedroom that used to be Esme's.

"Sixteen is the age witches and warlocks become adults. That's why you could stay in your van, and they never put you back into a foster home."

I turned back. "No, the reason they didn't put me back into a foster home was because I was smart and tired of being jerked around. I got my GED, got myself into college, and worked my butt off to become who I am. Without magic."

"And for that, your mother would be so proud."

I shrugged. "We may never know."

"If you help me, we might," Harriet said. "There's no indication your mother died. Whoever killed my mother may have abducted yours. She might still be alive."

"I'll believe that when I see it," I said, walking into my bedroom and closing the door before sliding to the floor and letting the tears flow down my cheeks.

1 4

I slept well besides the fact that I kept dreaming about people falling through trapdoors and dying. First, it was the woman who I'd seen fall. Then Harriet's mom—Ambeline. Then Emily.

When I woke up crying from my dream about Emily, it was half-past eleven, so I decided I'd had enough sleep.

Before showering, I needed to see if Esme's journal would reveal anything new to me. Something inside me needed her words.

I pushed the button by the baseboard and pulled the bookcase out of the way, revealing a wooden staircase that curved toward the attic. Penelope followed me up the stairs and into the warm, fairy-lit room. I sat in the oversized chair and grabbed Esme's worn journal from the side table.

The journal cracked a bit at the spine when I began flipping through pages.

I'd only been able to read a few passages as the

language in which Esme wrote the book was one I'd never seen before.

Part of me wondered if Harriet or Xander would have been able to read the language, but there was no way I would let someone else read Esme's journal, even if they could translate it. Plus, it seemed the journal revealed what I needed to know when I needed to know it.

As I flipped, a new readable page came into view. The entry was from fifty-some years before.

The house is complete. It took longer than expected, but I wanted to use more than my magic. I wanted to use my hands. My muscles. My lungs. My heart.

I wanted to incorporate my blood, sweat, and tears into my home.

In addition to my magic.

The pond was the hardest. Digging a magic pond without magic through the tough ground nearly broke me.

The trees are mere saplings now but will eventually grow large enough for treehouses, hammocks, and of course, shade. I can imagine my daughter and granddaughter enjoying the pond. Swimming in the summer. Skating in the winter. I hope they like them.

That was the end of what I could understand. The rest was still in the indecipherable language.

How had she known she would have a daughter and granddaughter?

I stood and looked out the window that faced the barn.

There were no trees. No pond.

It was dark, but the land was flat.

Could it be that I simply couldn't see the pond? I'd walked that bit of ground and hadn't gotten wet, but maybe my magic wasn't strong enough.

The only person I could talk to was Xander. He might have left in a hurry, but surely he'd take my call.

"Hello?" Xander sounded out of breath when he answered my call.

"It's Ellie," I said, trying not to be awkward.

"I know," he said. "What's wrong?"

"Do you think there are things I can't see because I don't know how to use my magic properly?"

He was silent on the other end.

"A woman came here this morning. A woman with magic."

This got his attention. "What do you mean a woman with magic came to your house this morning?"

"She's still here," I said. "Her name is Harriet Nightingale. She's staying in Dewdrop."

He mumbled a cuss word. "I'll be right over."

"You don't have to come over. She seems perfectly safe," I said. "I just want to know what I need to do to figure out my magic. To see things that might be there."

"What kind of things?"

I didn't know whether I should talk about the pond. What if I sounded like an idiot?

"What kind of things, El?"

"Like the pond and trees behind my barn?"

"Oh, that," he said.

"Are you saying there is?" I thought about this for a moment. "What else can't I see?"

"You can't force your magic," he said. "And her showing up there to try and get you to is not okay."

"She didn't try to get me to do anything," I said. "She's not here for me. She's here to solve a murder."

"What murder?" Xander growled.

"Her mother's," I said. "Apparently, she died the same way as the woman we saw fall through the trapdoor. Harriet thinks whoever did it was trying to kill her, not the other woman."

"Then you need to take that information to Jake," Xander said. "And kick her out of your house. If someone is trying to murder her, it's not safe to keep her there."

"So I should throw her out to be killed? I don't think so."

"You're too nice."

"I guess if not wanting someone to die is being too nice, then sure, I'm too nice." I paused. "I already feel like I'm responsible for one death. I don't want to be responsible for another."

"You are not responsible for that woman's death," Xander said. "Just because your hair changed doesn't mean you knew what to do with that information. If someone wanted you to stop a murder, they should have given you specific instructions."

His words made me feel slightly better.

"I'm coming over."

"No, no, no," I said. "Stop. I'm a big girl. I can handle myself. She's not dangerous. I might not know my magic very well, but my hair tells me she's safe." I hesitated, then asked, "Are there other things I can't see?"

"Yes," he said.

I could feel my forehead wrinkle with a frown, my hair buzz with suspicion. "How do you know what I can and can't see?"

He didn't respond immediately.

"Xander?"

"I just know. We've been places, and things have happened that you haven't noticed."

I tried to think of what he might be talking about, but if he'd seen things I hadn't, he'd been a good actor.

"Like what?"

"That's not for me to say. If you can't see something, I'm not supposed to point it out. Harriet has made an error, and if she doesn't follow the rules of magic, she's probably not someone you want to keep in your house."

"She's fine," I said. "I don't think she meant to. She knew I had magic because of my hair—and being Esme's granddaughter—but she spoke of the pond before she knew I didn't know of it." I paused to let Xander respond, but when he didn't, I continued, "That's why I need to figure it out. Learn my magic."

"You've had magic your whole life," Xander said, carefully. "But you only recently accepted it. Most accept it when they're children. But because your magic caused so much unhappiness, you pushed it away. It still got out when you were emotional. But the release of magic wasn't voluntary. Now, you're trying to get it out when it's used to huddling in the back corners of your mind. It's like a child that's been locked in a dark basement its entire life. It's going to be hesitant to come into the light."

As much as this made sense, it frustrated me.

I wanted to see.

To know.

If only I'd have embraced my magic when I was young. But if I had, I would have been made an outcast. The families who had kept me until my hair changed would never have given me the slightest chance.

"Fine," I said. "I'll wait."

"And be careful. You don't know this woman from Eve."

"Yeah, okay."

We hung up, and I hopped into the shower. I only had about ten minutes before the entire cast of the play would be in my studio.

15

W hen I opened the door to the barn, Katie and Melody stood in the middle of the floor, stretching in silence.

"Hey there," Katie said with a smile. "How are you?"

"I got some sleep," I said. "But I'm still pretty tired."

"She means because you saw someone die," Melody said. "That would mess me up."

Oh, oops. "Yeah, that was rough," I said. "I guess it seems like a lot has happened since then."

"Like what?" Katie asked.

I was about to tell her about Harriet when the door opened, and a bunch of people started filing in. "I'll tell you about it later," I shouted over the commotion.

The entire cast had gotten the memo of the venue change, but it took well over a half-hour to get the actual rehearsal moving. Everyone wanted to know what had happened at the theater and several people didn't show up at all. I tried to give some vague details, letting Katie and Melody fill in the rest.

"Let's start from the beginning and go through the entire play," Katie said. "I know the news said the snow isn't supposed to let up, but we will put on a show whether we have a full house or an empty one."

I guess I needed to get my line right one way or another.

The show began with Melody and a couple of the other women, but Bex and I weren't on stage during the opening scene.

"How are you doing?" Bex whispered so Katie wouldn't get mad that we were disrupting the rehearsal.

"I'm fine," I said. "Last night and this morning are a total blur. After the woman died, I came home, and Xander followed."

"Ooh," Bex said. "Why?"

"He thought someone was trying to break into the barn, but it was just me." I thought about this for a second. Maybe he'd known it was me all along and wanted to make sure I was okay. Or to spend time with me. Had he thought about kissing me from the get-go?

"Earth to Ellie," Bex said. "Spill."

"What?"

"You got a look on your face I've never seen before. What happened with you and Xander?"

I smiled, heat rising in my cheeks. "It was only to change my hair," I said.

"What was?"

"He kissed me," I said.

"It obviously worked," she said. "What color did it change?"

"White." I smiled. "Except it was like a shimmery white. Like snow crystals when they're hit by the sun."

"Then what happened?" Bex was literally on the edge of her seat.

"Nothing," I said. "He seemed to realize he needed to be somewhere and bolted."

"Oh." Bex slumped back in her chair.

"Oh?"

"I mean, I hoped it would have turned into a second kiss."

I had too, but I wasn't about to admit this to Bex.

"He seemed pretty adamant that it was only to change my hair."

"Mmm-hmm," Bex said. "That man looks at you with the biggest puppy dog eyes. He wanted to kiss you."

The thought made me a bit giddy inside.

"Ooh, I better get on stage," she said.

She hurried off, leaving me there with my feelings.

We were about halfway through the play when Harriet and Dylan Bram came into the barn.

The entire production stopped at the sight.

I walked over.

"This guy wouldn't stop pounding on your door," Harriet said.

"Where's Trinity?" Dylan said. He was wearing the same clothes he had been the night before, his hair was a mess, and his five o'clock shadow looked more like an eight o'clock shadow.

"She's not here," Melody said, stepping forward. "You know her reputation."

"That was one time," Dylan said. "She's never been late again."

Melody shrugged. "Either way, it's enough to get her kicked off this production. I have zero tolerance for tardiness."

"Look around," Dylan said. "She's not tardy. She's completely absent." He took a step toward Melody. "Is this because of last night? You know, you don't have to take out your rejection on her."

Melody's eyes widened. "This has nothing to do with last night."

"You're just jealous," Dylan spat. "You probably didn't tell her about the change in venue so you could kick her out of the play."

"I called her cell about ten times and left three voice-mails," Melody said. "Unlike your *girlfriend*, I'm a professional."

"Well, my *girlfriend* didn't come back to the room last night after she said she was going to rehearse with you."

Melody took a step toward him and pointed a finger in his chest. "You know perfectly well that I wasn't with her at the theater because you had to come and make your point about us not being together."

"Maybe she was with you after that."

"Or maybe she wasn't," Melody said. "I haven't seen Trinity since yesterday's rehearsal. Perhaps she's taken a page out of your playbook and found herself a different guy to hang out with."

"I'm calling Delilah," Dylan said.

"Don't bother," Melody said. "I already called her myself. She was next in line for the understudy role."

"You chose Delilah to replace Trinity?" Dylan tipped his head back and laughed. "You really can't take the pressure of someone being as good as you."

Melody took a deep breath. "I need some air." She walked out of the barn, leaving Dylan standing there.

I glanced at Katie, who looked angry as a cat in water.

The rest of the cast looked downright terrified.

"This has been great," Harriet finally said, pushing her glasses up on her nose. "But I think you should probably go since you didn't find your girlfriend." She grabbed Dylan's arm. He tried to wrench it away, but she was stronger than she appeared.

Dylan looked down at the teeny woman beside him in shock.

She was probably using some sort of magic and, though it probably shouldn't have, it made me smile.

"Fine, I'm leaving," Dylan said as if he had any choice in the matter. "But if you hear from Trinity, tell her I'm looking for her."

"I'm afraid no one will hear from Trinity," Jake said, appearing in the door in front of Harriet. "She's dead."

16

"What do you mean she's dead?" Dylan balled up his fists as if he might try to punch Jake.

"We ran the fingerprints of the woman who died last night in the trapdoor accident. They came back as Trinity's."

The words hit the entire room like a shock wave. Several people gasped, Dylan hit his knees as Harriet let go of his arm, and Katie stood looking at Jake as if someone had slapped her across the face.

I knew she might have been the one who had fallen, but I'd hoped it wasn't her.

"I'm sorry to have to announce it like this," Jake said. "We've notified her family. I knew she was supposed to be here for practice, and I didn't want you to worry."

"They weren't worried," Dylan said. His butt rested on his feet—feet that could have made the footprints we'd seen outside the theater. "How did she die?"

I tried to peek around to see if the bottom of his boots

had the star pattern, but I couldn't get a good enough angle to tell.

"The fall killed her," Jake said. "One of her ribs broke and pierced her heart."

"What about her face?" I asked.

Jake took a step toward Dylan and Deb, and another officer walked in behind him. "That's something we'd like to speak with Mr. Bram about."

Dylan stood, his eyes narrowed. "Why?"

"Standard procedure," Jake said.

"I wasn't even with Trinity last night," Dylan said, taking a step back.

"We're not saying you were," Jake said. "We simply want to ask you a few questions."

Dylan's eyes got all shifty and worried.

"Mr. Bram, please," Deb said. "Let's talk about this for a minute."

But Dylan apparently didn't want to answer their questions. He pushed past Jake and Deb, and though the other officer almost had him, he managed to wiggle free and take off outside.

I heard the rumble of a sports car in the driveway and then it sliding out onto the snowy gravel road.

Melody came back inside. "What was that all about?"

No one answered her question.

Jake sighed. "I had a feeling that might happen."

"Why did he run out of here like that?" Melody asked. "And why are you here, Jake?"

"The woman who died at the theater was Trinity," Jake said. "We believe Dylan might have had something to do with her death."

"Dylan might be an arrogant jerk, but he's not a murderer," Melody said. "He was with me last night. We got in a huge argument, but he was with me."

"What time was he with you?" I asked. "Because he was at the B&B right before Trinity died, but he had plenty of time to get to the theater and pull the lever."

"He was with me before that," Melody said. "Ask the girl at the front desk. I'm sure she'll remember where he was after you went to the theater."

It was a solid idea. I looked at Jake, and he nodded.

"Him running out of here doesn't exactly make him look innocent," Harriet said. "But I too am certain he didn't kill Trinity."

Jake turned to look at her. "And you are?"

"Harriet Nightingale." She held a hand out for him to shake. "The daughter of Ambeline Nightingale—the woman whose killer you let get away."

Jake's eyes widened.

Harriet continued, "And I'm here to figure out who murdered my mother. I believe the same person may be to blame for Trinity's murder."

Gasps came from all around me.

"Okay," I said. "Let's take this into the house." There was no need to get the rumor mill any more involved in this case than they already were.

"You can finish rehearsal without me, right?" I asked.

Katie nodded. "But you're going to have to say that line, eventually."

"I know," I said. "I will."

Jake, Harriet, and I went inside while Deb and the other officer tried to find Dylan.

"Let me begin by saying, it's nice to meet you in person," Jake said when we all sat at the table in the formal dining room.

"I'd like to say the same, but that would be a lie," Harriet replied.

Jake didn't seem too surprised by her response.

"I know you believe your mother was murdered, but we could not find any evidence to prove that was the case," Jake said. "Though, if you have additional evidence you'd like to provide connecting these two deaths, I'd be happy to take a look."

"I've sent you my evidence," Harriet said.

"And as I've told you," Jake said, "magical evidence does not hold up in a court of law."

"It should." Harriet looked out the window.

"But someone contacted you about meeting them at the theater last night, right?" I asked.

Harriet looked at me. "Yes."

"How did they contact you?" Jake asked.

"They sent a letter," Harriet said. "But there's no evidence on it."

"Would you mind if I looked, anyway?" Jake was being far more patient than I would have been with how difficult Harriet was being.

"I suppose," she said. "I'll be back."

When we heard her footsteps on the stairs, Jake said, "Is she staying here?"

"She showed up this morning," I said. "She was at the theater last night too. I think that's who was on the catwalk. She said someone told her they had information about her mother's death. She showed up, and

Trinity died. She thinks they were trying to kill her too."

"She's convinced this is part of a vendetta against her family." He glanced at the doorway. "She also thinks it has something to do with your mother's disappearance. It's how she originally hooked me into helping her. But the more I researched, the more it didn't line up."

"What about the charm?" I asked. "It's from a bracelet my mother wore."

Jake nodded his head slowly. "How did you know?"

"She showed me a picture. It was taken after I was born."

"How can you tell?"

"She's not pregnant in it, but she looks to be around the right age."

"And Harriet told you it was taken afterward, right?"

"Yes," I said.

"I'm not trying to make you feel stupid, but this is what she does. She plays on your feelings and gets you all wrapped up in her tale until you hit dead end after dead end. Sometimes it's hard to accept that someone could have died by accident."

"Do you think Trinity's death was an accident?"

"I'm not sure yet, but I'd say it's not." Jake looked at the doorway again, then lowered his voice. "The handle for the trapdoor was wiped clean of prints. If the construction workers had been trying to fix it, they would have had to handle it repeatedly. And, as you could tell from the mess backstage, they're not the best about cleaning up after themselves. I don't know why they'd wipe down a handle."

Made sense. "It could also have been magic," I said.

"Yes," he agreed. "It could have been. And what worries me is that Harriet is not only magical but desperate to find out something about her mother."

"You think she set this up to get the case reopened?"

"Weirder things have happened." Jake shrugged. "But I don't think she would have wiped down the handle either. Especially if she wants us to believe someone magical did it."

Harriet walked back into the room carrying a card-board banker's box.

"Here's the letter," Harriet said. "It's magical."

Jake put on a pair of gloves before picking it up. His expression didn't seem to indicate that he felt any magic coming off it.

"Why do you think it's magical?" Jake asked.

"I can feel it," Harriet said, handing him an envelope with the same handwriting on the address as was in the letter.

Jake put the letter back on the table and examined the envelope.

"I knew my mother died in a small town in Iowa, but until I got this last week, I couldn't remember the town name," she said. "I've been driving around the state since I was sixteen, going to every small-town theater I could find."

"But you've called me at least a dozen times," Jake said. "Didn't the receptionist say Cliff Haven Police Department when she answered the phone?"

"She probably did," Harriet said. "But it was always muffled. As was your phone number. It's untraceable. If you hadn't called my grandmother to inform her of my mother's death, we probably wouldn't have even had your number at all."

Jake shook his head like he didn't believe her. "So a week ago, the letter arrived revealing the name of our town?"

"Yes," she said. "And it was then that the fog seemed to lift. All those times I'd only heard muffled words from the receptionist, I could now remember her saying Cliff Haven Police Department."

I wasn't sure how Jake was taking this, but it sounded like magic to me.

"Then what?"

"Then I came to Cliff Haven," Harriet said. "Of course, I didn't make myself known. I'd been dying to find this town. At night, I'd sneak into the theater to look for clues. That's when I found this." She took the bracelet out of a small purple velvet bag and placed it on the table. "I believe you gave that to Emily."

Jake looked at the broken pieces with sadness in his eyes.

"And if this isn't what you call *real evidence* of Emily being there when my mother died," Harriet said. "I don't know what is."

Jake reached a hand out and picked up the pieces as gently as if they were a baby bird. "I bought it our senior year," Jake said. "Each charm meant something special."

I watched him turn them all in between his fingers.

"Okay," Jake said, closing his hand around the pieces. "Let's assume this is proof that Emily was there. You're saying she came back to Cliff Haven after leaving, having a baby, leaving the baby at a fire station, all without being seen by anyone who might recognize her?"

"She probably used her magic to disguise herself," Harriet said.

Hurt was written all over Jake's face at the thought of this. If she had come back after all that time and hadn't seen him, what did that mean?

"Maybe the bracelet was down there from before she had me," I said. "It could have broken at a different time."

Harriet pulled another picture out and pushed it across the table.

When I looked down, my breath caught in my chest.

The photograph was of Emily in a hospital bed, gazing down at a baby with stark white hair.

"She was wearing the bracelet when she had you," Harriet said.

17

I couldn't help the tears that came pouring down my cheeks. Emily looked so happy in the photo, gazing down at her brand-new baby—gazing down at me.

What happened? Why hadn't she kept me?

She wore a hospital bracelet alongside the silver one, but without a magnifying glass, I wasn't able to see what it said. And even with one, it was probably too pixelated to make anything out.

"Where was this taken?" I asked. "And how did you get it?"

"My mother took it," Harriet said. "I was there too."

"You were there when Ellie was born?" Jake asked.

"I was only a toddler," Harriet said. "I don't remember it, but there's a picture of me holding you."

"Why were you there?" I asked. "Why was your mother? Were they friends?"

Harriet looked at Jake, who said, "You need to tell her."

"Tell me what?" I asked, looking between the two of them.

"They weren't merely friends," Harriet finally said. "They were sisters."

"Sisters?" I tried to keep my emotions level, but I could feel my scalp tingle. "How?"

"They had the same father," Jake said. "A rather horrible man, if you ask me."

"I won't deny that," Harriet said. "Though I never met him."

"He left town long before either of you were born," Jake said. "I don't know where he is now."

"He's dead," Harriet said.

"That means we're cousins?" I asked, still trying to wrap my head around everything. I glanced back down at the photo. My mother was breathtakingly beautiful with her white hair pulled back into a messy bun, a couple of ringlets hanging down toward her face. Her cheeks were rosy, probably from giving birth, and her lips were full.

When I looked up, Jake was staring at the photo too.

"Do you know who my father is?" I asked.

Harriet looked at me then at Jake then back again. "I assumed it was him."

I sighed, and Jake shook his head.

"I guess I was wrong?"

"Emily and I never had that kind of relationship," Jake said.

"Then do you have a twin brother? Because Ellie looks a lot like you." Harriet laughed, but neither of us joined.

"She doesn't look at all like me," Jake said. "Other than the eyes, she looks identical to Emily."

How hard must it have been for him to see her—the woman he loved more than anything in the world—in me?

"If my mother or grandmother were alive, I'd ask them if they knew, but they're both gone." Harriet huffed. "And we need to find out who killed my mother. If we do, we might figure out what happened to Emily too."

Jake had warned me about not buying into Harriet's story, but when I glanced up at him, he looked like he wasn't taking his own advice.

"What other evidence do you have?" Jake asked.

"I thought you'd never ask," Harriet said, pulling so many things out of the box it was a wonder they all fit inside. "You've seen these—they're photos from the original crime scene."

"How did you get those?" Jake asked.

Harriet waved a hand in his face. "It doesn't matter." She grabbed one in particular. "If you look at how she landed, it's in the same position as the girl who died last night."

"They both fell through the same hole," Jake said. "And they were both around the same size, so that's purely physics."

"Wait," I said before Harriet could take the photo away. "This one looks different than the crime scene last night." I studied the photo. "What is it?"

"There have been updates made to the stage," Jake said. "When Ambeline died, Katie had the hole closed up. I'd assume there's more dust and grime down there now."

That wasn't it, but I couldn't put my finger on what it was either. "I don't know, it might come to me later."

Harriet continued, showing us picture after picture of

the crime scene, describing how only magic could have made the stage fall like it did, and going back to the letter that had magically come to her only a week before.

"Is magic traceable?" I asked.

"Some magic is," Harriet said. "Why?"

"Because if you could trace the magic in the letter back to who sent it, you might be able to figure out who did all this."

Harriet nodded. "I tried that."

"Then I'm out of ideas," I said, peeking at the crime scene photo of Harriet's mother's body. My hair tingled. I was missing something.

"I could try to lift some fingerprints off the paper," Jake said. "But I'm guessing I won't find much."

"Speaking of," I said. "Why do you think the person didn't send you the letter before now?"

"I have an idea," Harriet said. "But it's not fully fleshed out yet."

"Can we help?" Jake asked.

Harriet sighed. "I think whoever killed my mother and took Emily did so because of the family line."

Jake and I didn't say anything.

"I think our grandfather had another child at some point," she said. "And since our grandfather was one of the most powerful warlocks of his day, there's quite a legacy he will leave for someone. With both of our mothers out of the way, this other person thought they'd try to get rid of us too. But you were in foster care, and they might not know you exist."

"But why can't the legacy extend to multiple people?" I

asked. "Why do you have to die? Is it about money or something?"

"It's more than money when it comes to magic." Harriet looked out the window. "Whoever remains will receive their portion of his magic."

"But you said he already died, so shouldn't the magic have already been disbursed?" Jake asked.

"I believe it's been put in a temporary holding until things get situated," Harriet said.

"Like who lives and who dies?" I sat back in my chair a bit. "This doesn't mean only one of us can live, does it?"

Harriet laughed. "No. It means if you and I are the sole survivors, we'll be able to split the magic."

"But it sounds like we're not," I said.

"I believe there's one other," she said. "A grandson—our cousin—who wants the magic all to himself."

"And my mother," I said.

"Yes," Harriet said. "But I believe he has made her magic obsolete."

"I thought you said you didn't think she was dead," I said.

"I don't." Harriet sighed. "There are other ways to remove magic than death."

Like locking it in your mind basement your entire life.

"So, you think he's the one who is trying to kill you?" I asked. "Our other cousin?"

"Yes," she said. "When our grandfather died last week, I got the letter. I don't think that's a coincidence. Magic can only be held temporarily."

"How long?" Jake and I asked at the same time.

"It depends, but let's say this guy is desperate,"

Harriet said. "And when he finds out Emily had a child too, you'll be next."

I gripped the edge of the table. This was a lot for my mind to take in. "What if I just agree to give up my portion of the magic? It's not like I need it."

Harriet looked at me like I was insane. "You might not need it, but it's rightfully yours."

I smiled. "Seriously, I have everything I've ever dreamed of here. I have friends, a home, and now I have you—family."

Harriet's eyes widened. "I never considered you'd be content with this. With me as your family."

"Well, I am," I said. "And if I knew who this warlock cousin was, I'd tell him that too."

"Good luck," Harriet said. "He'd probably kill you before he'd hear you out."

Jake gaped at her, then looked at his phone. "They found Dylan," he said. "They're taking him to the station. Do you want to come down and talk to him with me?"

I glanced at Harriet.

"It's a dead end," Harriet said. "He didn't kill Trinity."

"It may be," Jake said. "But the thing about police work is that we have to follow every angle."

"Suit yourself," she said, then looked at me. "When you get back, we can talk further."

"Sounds good." I looked down at the picture on the table. "Do you mind if I keep this?"

Harriet glanced at the photo of my mother holding newborn me. "Sure, go ahead."

When I picked it up, my entire chest warmed, and I could feel the tingle in my hair. "I think I'll frame it."

18

I drove separately from Jake. As we pulled into the police station, I squeezed Mona's steering wheel. "My mom loved me," I said aloud. "I could see it in her eyes."

Mona's metal steering wheel with tiny lilac flowers carved into it seemed to electrify only slightly beneath my hands. Almost like she was telling me she was listening and happy for me.

It was probably because I'd never had a real family, but sometimes I would have sworn Mona and Penelope could actually communicate with me. Well, more than a normal van or pig would have been able to.

I locked Mona's driver's side door—the rest of the doors were always locked—before following Jake into the station and back to an interrogation room. I'd only ever been in one of the conference rooms and Jake's office.

This room was cold with a concrete floor, four metal chairs, and a two-way mirror on one wall like in TV shows. The table was metal and bolted to the ground with a metal pole elevated about four inches off the top to secure suspects with handcuffs.

The air smelled like urine and disinfectant.

"Dylan Bram," Jake said. "I believe we've met."

Dylan nodded.

"And this is Ellie Vanderwick, one of Cliff Haven's consultants."

"She's the town witch, right?"

Jake didn't take the bait. "We know you were at the theater last night around the time Trinity fell through the trapdoor." Jake opened a file and took out a picture of Trinity crumpled beneath the stage.

Dylan glanced at it and paled. "I didn't do that. I wouldn't hurt anyone."

"When was the last time you saw Trinity?" Jake asked.

I glanced at the photo. It looked exactly how I remembered it besides the lighting. It was obviously from the flash of a camera rather than a tiny cell phone app flashlight.

"I saw her after rehearsal," he said. "She and Melody had gotten into an argument. I think Katie told her something about working harder to get the role. As if she would give the role to someone other than her own daughter."

"But Katie did give Trinity a role once over Melody," I said.

Jake nodded. "I do believe that was because of you." He looked at Dylan.

"What can I say? Women want to be with me." He sat back, crossed his ankle over his knee, and put his hands behind his head. "Even Melody to this day wants to be with me. She was so mad Trinity got the movie role over her. I bet that's why she killed Trinity. That, and because she was jealous of me and Trinity being together."

His entire demeanor was gross. Sure, he was good-looking, but that was about all he had going for him. "Melody didn't want to be with you. Up until a couple days ago, she was in a relationship."

"A sham relationship," Dylan said. "Everyone knew it was only for publicity."

"Let's go back to the last time you saw Trinity," Jake said.

"I just told you, I saw her after rehearsal—when Katie told her she could take Melody's role. So she went back over to the theater to practice with Melody."

"And when exactly did you go over to the theater to talk to Melody?" I asked. "Because I find it hard to believe that Trinity would have approved of the idea of you spending one-on-one time with your ex-girlfriend. But if they were practicing together . . ."

"I mean, I don't know if they were practicing *together*," Dylan said. "That's just what Trinity said. But I went to see Melody about an hour after Trinity left."

"So you went to talk, and then what?" Jake asked, taking notes.

"We didn't talk much," Dylan said. "She mostly yelled and threw things."

"Where did this take place?" I asked, remembering the state of the dressing room.

"The office upstairs," Dylan answered. "She threw a pen and a sticky pad. Nothing that actually hurt."

"What was she yelling about?" Jake asked.

"Me being with Trinity. Trinity getting her role. You know, stupid stuff." Dylan shifted in his seat. "Other than that, I have nothing to tell you. Melody and I got in a fight. I went out the side door and back to the B&B. You saw me there."

"Flirting with the staff," I said.

"Flirting is harmless," Dylan said.

"Can I see the bottom of your boots?" I asked.

He looked at me, then at Jake.

Jake nodded.

"Why do you care about the bottom of my boots?" Dylan asked.

"I would like to confirm that you went out the side door as you stated," I said.

"If you saw footprints, they weren't mine," he said. "The snow would have covered them by the time you got to the theater."

"Please show us the bottom of your boots," Jake said. "Otherwise, we can take them into evidence, and you probably won't get them back anytime soon."

"These are expensive boots," Dylan said. "Fine." He lifted one foot onto the table.

I leaned forward to look, my breath held.

But the sole was a plain striped pattern—no stars to be found.

"Do you own any other boots?" I asked.

"A couple," Dylan said. "But I only brought the one pair here."

"Have you ever seen a pair of boots with stars on the bottom?" I asked.

He nodded. "Trinity was obsessed with them. Langlin boots."

"Did Trinity have a pair?" I asked.

"A few pairs, but she didn't bring any of them with her," he said.

Jake wrote this down.

"Was everything okay with you and Trinity?" I asked. "You don't seem very broken up about her death."

"It sucks she died," Dylan said. "But if she wasn't so set on beating Melody at every single thing, she wouldn't have been rehearsing so late."

"Other than Melody, do you know if she was going to the theater to meet anyone?" I asked. "Maybe someone who had the same hair color as she did?"

"Same hair color?" Dylan laughed. "And what color is that? Her real hair color—which no one really knows, by the way? Or her dyed hair? Or the wig?"

"Well, I was talking about the orange wig," I said. "But . . ."

Jake pulled out another photo—one of Trinity on a metal table. With blonde hair. Just like in the mural.

It had been warning me, and I'd failed.

I dropped my head.

Jake continued the questioning. "Do you know anyone she might have been meeting at the theater regardless of hair color?"

"No one other than Melody," Dylan said. "And honestly, it's crazy there were so many people in one place with such ugly hair. Trinity's wig order got all messed up, so I understand why she was wearing it, but two other people too?"

I didn't mention there were actually three other people with the same color hair—me, Trinity, Harriet, and the mysterious yeller.

"Before Trinity fell through the trapdoor," I said. "Another woman was yelling at her about something she deserved. Something she should have gotten."

Dylan looked at me like I was a complete idiot. "It had to be Melody. About the movie role," he finally said. "She could have been wearing a wig, too, you know."

I thought about it for a minute. The woman could have been Melody, but the voice didn't sound like Melody's voice. Though she was an actress, so maybe?

We sat in silence for a few minutes before Jake went another direction in the questioning. "Do you know how Trinity got all the bruising on her face?"

"Not from me," Dylan said. "It was probably whoever was at the theater that night." Dylan paused. "And I feel like the answer is pretty obvious."

Jake and I waited for Dylan to make his accusation.

"Melody," Dylan finally said in an exasperated tone. "I know you don't want to see it, but Melody is your murderer. She hated Trinity since they were teenagers. Trinity got her job, her boyfriend, and was going to take her role in her own mother's play. She couldn't have that happen. So, she put on a wig and killed her competition."

My mind flew back to her and Bonnie, conspiring in whispers after the last rehearsal. Bonnie wouldn't have suggested Melody do anything to hurt Trinity. Would she?

19

J ake and I left Dylan in the interrogation room and headed down the hall toward Jake's office. I'd only been in there briefly once before, but this time, I could take it all in. Including a candid picture of him and Emily from what looked like a carnival.

Certainly, he'd dated since my mother disappeared over twenty years before. I couldn't imagine how those women would have felt if they had walked into his office and saw a photo of him with his old flame. He probably put it away when he was in a relationship.

"That's a good picture," I said. "You look happy."

"And young," he said, picking it up. "Your mom was something else. She convinced me to go on the Ferris wheel, even though she knew I was afraid of heights. It was one of our first dates—I finally convinced her to go out with me—and I didn't want to do anything to make her not like me. But then I nearly cried at the top when it stopped to let other people on."

I laughed.

"I thought she would think I was stupid, but she held my hand and told me it was going to be okay. Her touch always soothed me." He put the photo back on the desk behind him. "She never made me go on a Ferris wheel again."

"It's kind of exciting to think she might still be out there somewhere, right?"

His smile drooped. "I don't want you to get your hopes up," he said. "Harriet has some convincing information, but I've found nothing to believe Emily was there the night of Ambeline's death."

"Do you have pictures from Ambeline's case?"

He nodded, then turned to a file cabinet behind him and pulled out a file so big it had to be held together by an extra-thick rubber band. "What would you like to see?"

"Wow," I said. "Is every murder file that big?"

"Death," Jake corrected. "We never concluded she died by homicide."

"Right."

"But no," he said. "Most of this is stuff Harriet has sent us over the years. Though, how she got it to us if she didn't even know where our town was is beyond me." He opened the file and pulled out a couple of old photos from the front. "Is this what you're looking for?"

I wasn't sure what I was looking for, but there was something there.

"Can I compare them to the ones you have of Trinity?"

He handed me the other file he'd had in the interrogation room.

I placed the photos of the women lying beneath the stage next to one another and studied them.

Both women were in strikingly similar positions, which probably meant they both fell the same way. Ambeline's face wasn't bruised and broken like Trinity's.

Then it hit me.

"These were taken from different angles," I said. "And the lighting is different."

"Ambeline's was taken from the stage through the trapdoor," Jake said. "The lighting is from the stage lights. Whereas Trinity's was taken below the stage with a flash."

"Right," I said. "Because the door closed again after Trinity fell through."

"That was part of the reason we thought it was an accident—perhaps part of Renard's Curse—because if you're going to let someone fall through the floor, why wouldn't you close the hatch? It would make it less likely for someone to find the body until you were far away from the scene."

"Who called in about Ambeline's crime?"

"Katie," Jake said. "She found her when she was getting ready to start a rehearsal."

"Did Ambeline live around here?"

"No," he said. "She visited a couple of times after Emily disappeared, then I didn't see her here again. Until this."

"I wonder if she helped Emily disappear?" I glanced back at the picture behind him. It was still shocking that Emily had gotten pregnant, left me at a fire station, and disappeared.

"If Ambeline and Harriet were there when you were born, Ambeline probably knew something."

"Do you think Emily could have been here when Ambeline died?"

Jake looked down at the photo. "If that bracelet had been there that night, we would have found it."

"Which could mean she went there afterward," I said.

"Or it could mean Harriet is setting us up."

I hadn't wanted to hear that, but I knew it was entirely possible.

"Chief?" Deb poked her head into the office. "Dylan's lawyer is here demanding he be charged or released."

"Already?" Jake asked.

Deb shrugged. "We have nothing to charge him with, so I let him go."

Jake stood and walked out of his office past Deb and me. We followed.

Dylan was still in the lobby when we got there.

"I would ask you not to leave town, but the road conditions have worked that out for me," Jake said.

Dylan's lawyer looked at Dylan and said, "Keep quiet." Then she turned to Jake. "We have no intention of leaving until the judge permits it."

Dylan nodded once. The two of them were about to walk out the doors when he turned back. "You didn't hear this from me, but Melody told me she was going to kill Trinity when we were arguing."

Dylan's lawyer tugged on his arm.

"Ouch," he said. "What? It's true. She was mad and said if I didn't leave Trinity, she'd kill us both."

The lawyer sucked in a breath and let it out. "Let's go," she said.

"It's okay," Jake said when they were gone. "I'm about ninety percent confident he didn't kill Trinity."

Deb looked at him. "Where does the ten percent come in?"

"We need to talk to the woman he was with at the B&B," I said. "He was with her before Trinity's death and after. If they were together the entire time, he'd be innocent. But we need to get to her before Dylan does."

2 0

The woman wasn't working, but Jake knew where she lived.

When we pulled up to the tiny house, a compact car was in the driveway.

"Hey," she said when she opened the door. "Is everything okay?"

"Can we come in?" Jake asked.

I peeked into the house through the slit of the open door. It looked like she might have had a child with all the toys on the floor.

"The baby's sleeping," she said. "Do you mind if I come out instead?"

It was getting dark, and the chill made her shiver.

"This won't take long," Jake said. "Can you tell us what happened the night of Trinity's death?"

She nodded. "I was working at the front desk when Trinity and Dylan came down the stairs so fast I thought a herd of elephants was attacking," she said. "They were obviously in an argument, and Trinity left in a huff. Dylan didn't follow, but probably an hour later, he left too. When he came back, he and I started talking."

"And how long did you talk?" Jake asked.

I stood back a bit, unsure if she recognized me as the woman who had seen them together.

"Only for a few minutes," she said.

"And in that few minutes, did anything happen?"

"Someone came in to check in, and then another lady came in looking for Trinity." She peeked around Jake. "That was you, wasn't it? Only your hair was different."

"It changes," I said.

"Yeah." She turned her attention back to Jake. "I know."

Her boss, Belinda, wasn't a huge fan of mine even though I'd impressed her a bit by solving a murder recently. That entire family basically hated me, including one of Bex's friends, Laura.

"Then what happened?" Jake asked.

"He went back up to their room," she said. "It wasn't until the police cars showed up that he came back down, and we went outside to see what was going on."

Jake considered this for a minute. "Is there any way to get out of the upstairs rooms without going past the front desk?"

The woman nodded, her teeth chattering slightly. "There are fire escapes attached to every room and a back entrance goes out to the alley."

"So you don't know whether he stayed in his room that entire time?" Jake asked.

She gaped at him. "I—uh—no," she said. "But he

didn't kill her, if that's what you're asking. He's so nice and sweet. I don't think he'd hurt a fly."

"We don't need to take any more of your time," Jake said.

"One more question," I said as she turned to walk back inside. "Did you see Trinity's face before she stormed out?"

The woman thought about it for a minute. "It all happened so fast. She was freaking out. But, no." She shook her head. "I don't think I did."

"Okay, thanks," I said.

When she was back in her house, Jake said, "Let's go look at the B&B. Deb already did a preliminary search of Trinity's room and found nothing, but we should take another look. We might be able to determine whether Dylan left the room that night."

"Or if he has any boots with stars on the bottom."

Belinda smiled at Jake when he walked in, but her smile faltered when she saw me. "Doing some more investigating, are we?"

"We need to check Trinity's room one more time and the exit that goes to the alley," Jake said.

"Be my guests," Belinda said, handing him the key to the room. "Just so you know, Mr. Hot Stuff is in the room next door with Trinity's friend. He seemed pretty upset when he got here."

"Interesting," Jake said.

"You got any feelings about this one?" Belinda asked me.

"Not yet," I said. "But we'll see."

"Ellie's so much more than her feelings," Jake said. "She's a smart cookie. And an observant one too."

"Wonder where she gets that from," Belinda muttered.

"Emily, I'm sure," Jake said, putting a point on the fact that I couldn't have gotten it from him.

Even though it was common knowledge that Jake wasn't my father, most of the town thought he was anyway.

"Let me know if you need anything," Belinda said with a smile.

Jake and I headed upstairs to the room Trinity had been staying in. When he opened the door, the room was in pristine check-in ready condition other than a few suitcases, shoes, and a purse in the corner.

"Do you think the maid service came in after the officers were here?" I asked. "Or was it like this before?"

"The maids must have come in," Jake said. "We hadn't officially cleared the scene, but they probably didn't get the memo."

I walked to the window and checked for the fire escape. It was a small platform with a ladder that extended down to the alley. "He probably could have gotten out here," I said. "But any footprints will have been covered with snow at this point."

Jake was still looking around the room. "None of these boots have stars on the soles."

"Good to know." I tried to open the window but

couldn't. "On second thought," I said. "This window is painted shut. I don't think he got out this way."

Jake tried and confirmed. "Yeah, it's stuck." He looked around. "I don't think there's anything else to be gleaned from this room. Especially, since it's been cleaned."

"Is her family going to pick up her belongings?" I asked.

"I think so," Jake said.

I glanced at the suitcase and the purse stacked on top. "Do you think the officers went through the contents?"

Jake squinted his eyes as if trying to remember. "I don't know if they made it that far."

"Think we should look?"

"Probably," Jake said. "You take the purse. I'll take the suitcase." He handed me a pair of gloves and pulled on his own pair.

I picked up the heavy, oversized purse and took it to the freshly made bed. Carefully, I sorted through the contents. Chapstick, a hairbrush, sunglasses, more makeup than I'd use in an entire lifetime, and—

"Oh," I said. "I think you should deal with this one."

Jake hurried over. "What?"

"There's a gun in there."

Jake pulled out the gun and set it on the bed. "Anything else in there of note?"

I pulled a letter out and handed it to him. "Like, literally of note?" I laughed.

He shrugged. "Read it since it's already been opened."

I pulled out a card that seemed nice enough on the front, but inside was a different story. "I think you're going to want to see this too."

Jake took the card and read it aloud. *"That role should have gone to me, and you know it. Watch your back."* He turned it over. "Was it addressed?"

I shook my head and handed him the envelope. "But whoever sent it has incredibly neat handwriting." It was almost a script-type font with an oversized oval to dot the i. "And it says something similar to what the other woman with orange hair was yelling at her."

"We'll check it all for prints," he said. "There wasn't anything of note in the suitcase."

He locked the room back up, leaving the gun and letter for the on-duty officers he'd called to collect as evidence.

At the end of the hall furthest from the lobby was a staircase that led straight down to a door.

The door easily pushed open and led out to the alley. Parked dead center in the barely plowed alleyway was a sports car with the license plate DLNBRAM.

"Looks like he's familiar with this exit," I said.

"Which means if we take prints off this door, his will be on them. But we won't know from when." Jake walked outside further and glanced down the length of the alley.

"Is it even legal to park here?" I asked.

A smile broke over Jake's face. "You know what, it's not."

21

J ake was on the phone with a towing company when a shadow passed beneath a streetlight at the end of the alley.

"I'll be right back," I said. Whoever was over there was acting suspiciously, trying to move in the shadows.

When I came around the corner, someone dressed in all black with a black hat and dark sunglasses looked back at me and then took off running.

If there was one thing I was good at, it was running. My boots weren't the perfect shoes for the job, but they didn't stop my legs from pumping. By the time the person made it through the trees into the middle of the square, I was on their heels.

I reached out and grabbed the hat off their head, revealing a gorgeous head of blonde hair. "Melody?"

Melody whipped around and faced me.

"Why are you running from me?" I looked back. "And why were you sneaking around in the shadows?"

"It's none of your business," she said. "You're not a cop."

I handed her the hat. "You're right. I'm not." I took a step back. "But you're a suspect in this murder case."

"They already questioned me and let me go."

"But do you have an alibi?" I asked. "Other than you were in the theater's office, had an argument with Dylan, threw some things at him, and threatened to kill him and Trinity after you found out she was the one who got the movie role over you?"

"Who told you that?"

"Dylan," I said. "He's telling everyone you did it. And when you act suspicious, it looks like he might be telling the truth." A thought popped into my head. "Did you send Trinity a threatening note?"

"Why would you think that?"

"Because you were mad she took your role?"

Melody laughed. "Did you find something in her room?"

I stared at her.

"Wait, you did?" she asked, then stopped to think about it. "What did it say?"

"I'm not going to tell you," I said.

"Was it specifically about the role?"

"Yes," I said. "Why?"

"I wasn't the only one up for that role. I didn't even know Trinity was in the running," Melody said. "Any of those other women could have sent that note."

"It doesn't matter. Jake's going to take fingerprints, so we'll know for sure."

"Good," she said. "It'll prove my innocence once and for all."

I stared at her. My hair told me she wasn't dangerous, but it could have been that she just wasn't dangerous to me.

"You don't think I'd actually kill someone because they stole my role and dated my ex-boyfriend, do you?" she asked.

"It sounds like good motive," I said.

"What about—what about—" She snapped her fingers as if trying to think of someone else who might be to blame. "That little redhead. She was at the theater that night too."

"Harriet?" I asked. "How did you know she was there?"

"She asked if she could be," Melody said. "She could have pulled the lever."

"It's entirely possible," I said. "What did Bonnie tell you to do to Trinity?"

Melody's eyes widened. "What do you mean?"

"When the two of you were whispering the other day after rehearsal?" I asked.

"She didn't tell me to kill Trinity, if that's what you're asking."

"Maybe you intended to injure her," I said. "You were one of only a handful of people who knew the trapdoor was being fixed."

"You can believe whatever you want to believe," Melody said. "I didn't do it. I didn't try to hurt her. I didn't kill her. I can get roles on my own merit."

"If you didn't do it, who did?"

"Beats me," she said. "It could have been one of the other actresses on the list."

"If it was one of them, do you think they'll be after you next?"

She laughed. "There's no way I'm getting that role. I'm too fit—as if that's even a thing in Hollywood."

"I'm sorry. I didn't mean to—"

"I should go home."

"That's probably a good idea."

"Don't tell anyone I was out here, okay?" she asked. "I don't want them to get the wrong idea."

I didn't agree.

"Please?"

"What were you doing out here in the first place dressed like you're going to rob a bank?"

"That is none of your business," she said.

"Then I promise nothing," I said. "In fact, I think Jake should know what you were doing."

She glared at me. "You would seriously do that to me? To Katie?"

I sighed. "Look, I don't think you're doing anything wrong."

"Then you'll keep it quiet, no questions asked."

She turned and walked in the opposite direction of the B&B without looking back at me.

When I returned to the alleyway behind the B&B, a tow truck driver had already hooked up Dylan's car and was pulling it onto the flatbed.

Jake stood to the side watching as Dylan and a woman I didn't recognize took turns yelling at Jake and the tow truck driver.

I felt like I needed to do something, but who was I to get in the middle of it?

Thankfully, I didn't have to.

Belinda came storming around the corner. Behind the desk, she looked like any other sweet B&B host, but as she marched toward Dylan, there was nothing sweet about her. Her face was red, her fists were balled, and her voice was loud, "That. Is. Enough!"

Dylan and the woman stopped yelling, their faces both shocked. It was then that I recognized her. She was the brunette holding Dylan's hand with her head on his shoulder when I'd come out of the theater after Trinity had fallen.

"This is a place of business," Belinda said in a normal voice. "I will not let you tarnish my good name by standing out here hollering."

"We're very sorry," the woman said. "We won't be yelling any longer."

The tow truck driver had finished getting the car on the flatbed and hopped into the cab. Before he closed the door, he said to Jake, "I'll take it to the impound lot."

Jake nodded. "Thanks."

"You're seriously impounding my car," Dylan said, careful to keep his voice down.

"You parked in a no-parking area," Jake said, pointing to the sign that clearly stated it was a tow-away zone. "It was blocking the flow of traffic."

"That's absurd," Dylan said, waving his arms around. "There is no traffic back here."

"Not right now," Belinda said. "But in the morning, there will be. This alley is where all the local businesses get deliveries. If you didn't act like such an entitled little baby, you'd care about the town you grew up in. Sure, you're hot stuff, and all the girls are gaga over you, including my staff. God help them. But the minute you're gone, we'll go back to normal, and you'll be a memory again. Now, do you want that memory to be a good one or a bad one?" She crossed her arms over her chest.

Dylan huffed, but something about his expression changed. It was like he actually took what she said to heart.

"Come on, let's go inside," the woman grabbed Dylan's arm and pulled him back toward the door that led upstairs directly to the room.

"No," Dylan said. "I need to get this sorted out. I can't not have a car."

"Feel free to come by the station first thing tomorrow morning," Jake said.

"What do you want to know?" Dylan asked. "Are you going to keep towing my car until I give you some sort of information?"

The woman next to him said, "You shouldn't be talking to them without your lawyer."

"Stop, Delilah," he said. "I need my car back."

"My father could get you a car in an hour," she said.

"I want my car, not some beat-up junker from your daddy's lot," Dylan said. "But the only way to do that is to give the police information."

"I'm not trying to blackmail you into telling me anything," Jake said. "I was simply towing a vehicle that was parked improperly."

"Dude, the license plate spells out my name," Dylan said. "I mean, like, not really my name. But sort of. You know what I mean."

"It doesn't matter," Jake said. "If it had been Ellie's van, I would have towed it too."

I glanced over and wondered if that was the truth. Or would he have given me a warning first? Either way, I wouldn't find out. I was a law-abiding citizen.

"Look, I wasn't with Trinity. I wasn't in the theater at all after Melody and I fought. I came back here and flirted with the front desk lady. Then I went back outside when the police cars came." He glanced over his shoulder. "I didn't even know they were there for Trinity."

"So, you were with the woman from the front desk the entire time?" I asked.

"Yes," Dylan said. "She can tell you."

"She did tell us," I said. "She said you went back up to your room and then came back down when the police cars showed up."

Dylan's gaze darted to Belinda, then back to me. "Uh, yeah."

"So then you weren't together the entire time." I had a feeling I knew where this was going.

Dylan glanced at Delilah, then said, "I don't want to get her in trouble for leaving her post," Dylan said. "But if it's between that and me going to prison for murder, I'm saving myself. She and I went up to my room—"

"Trinity's room," Delilah corrected, a disgusted look crossing her face.

"Yeah, okay, Trinity's room," Dylan said. "And we, well, you know. But it was fast, and then she was right back to work."

Belinda rolled her eyes. "That's what I get for hiring hormonal young folks."

"But it proves I wasn't there," Dylan said.

"Only if she'll corroborate your story," Jake said. "Which she might do if she knew she wouldn't be fired."

Belinda nodded. "I'm not going to fire someone for a minor lapse. She's been a good employee until Mr. Hot Stuff came back to town, and she'll be a good employee again the moment he's gone. I'll talk to her about it and see if her story lines up."

"Thank you," Jake said.

"But as for you," Belinda turned her attention to Dylan. "The minute I get you off the hook for this, I want you gone. You've done nothing but cause pain in this town. Melody might not be perfect, but she's a true Cliffer, and we Cliffers stick together—something your parents should have taught you when you were young."

"Deal," Dylan said. "I'll leave Cliff Haven and never come back. The girls are hotter in Poppy Hills, anyway." He winked at Delilah. She blushed. I sighed.

"I have one more question," I said as Dylan and Delilah turned to walk away. "Was anyone threatening Trinity?"

Dylan and Delilah both whipped around to face me.

"Not that I'm aware of," Dylan said, looking at Delilah. Delilah shook her head no.

"Why?" Dylan asked.

"We found a threatening note in her purse along with a gun," Jake said. "We think whoever did this might be responsible."

"It wouldn't be the first time she's gotten a note like that," Delilah said. "It's not uncommon to get threatening letters when you're an up-and-coming star."

"What about the gun?" I asked. "Do you know why she would have been carrying it?"

"Trinity's always carried a gun," Delilah said. "Since we were old enough to get our conceal and carry, she had a gun on her."

"How long have you and Trinity been friends?" I asked.

"Since we were in high school." Delilah looked down at her feet. "She was my best friend. I can't believe she's gone."

"Not to be insensitive," I said. "But where were you the night Trinity died, Delilah?"

"I was in Des Moines. Shopping." Delilah wiped a tear from her cheek.

"When did you get into town?" Jake asked.

"Right before the police showed up at the theater," Delilah said. "I have receipts from the shopping trip." She pulled a wallet out of her purse and handed a receipt to Jake.

I peeked over Jake's shoulder to see the receipts, but in the dark, it was hard to make anything out.

"Do you mind if I keep these?" Jake asked.

"Not at all," Delilah said.

"I think that's all we have," Jake said. "Thank you for talking to us."

Jake and I walked back around to our vehicles.

"Are you one hundred percent certain now?" I asked when we were out of earshot of the others.

"There's no evidence to hold him. I can't make him stay in town." Jake sighed. "The problem is, the most likely suspect isn't someone I want to arrest."

"Who?" I was pretty certain he was talking about Melody, but I didn't want to assume and sound stupid.

"Melody," he said, his voice hushed.

"I don't think she did it," I said, contemplating whether I should tell him Melody was in the alley earlier.

"I know it was her who you ran after," Jake said. "I saw her sneaking around when we walked outside."

"Do you think she was up to something?" I asked.

"I don't know," he said. "Do you?"

My hair told me she wasn't, but my common sense told me it wasn't that simple. "I don't know."

22

W hen I got home, Penelope and Harriet sat on the couch together, watching a documentary about people living in the wilderness.

Penelope snuggled up next to me when I plopped down, exhaustion taking over.

"Did you figure out it wasn't him?" Harriet said.

"I think so," I said.

"One down, how many to go?"

"Two or three, I guess," I said. "Maybe four, if what you're saying is real."

"Melody and me, and who else?"

I shrugged. "And about a half-dozen women who all wanted the same Hollywood role."

Harriet turned the TV off, and Penelope let out a grunt as if she was actually watching it.

"You can follow all these leads," Harriet said. "But none of them will pan out."

I was too tired to debate it with her. "Let's talk about

it tomorrow," I said, standing. I set Penelope on the ground, and she hurried out the piggy door to do her business one last time before bed.

Harriet stood. "Are you still okay with me staying here? Even though I'm a suspect in a murder investigation?"

"I figure if you wanted to kill me, you would have done so by now." I laughed, but Harriet's face remained neutral. "It was a joke."

"I'm aware," Harriet said, still not breaking a smile. "However, I don't think you understand the power this house holds."

Another topic I wasn't ready to get into when all I wanted to do was sleep. But this one, Harriet wasn't going to drop. I could sense it like I could sense my hair drooping and turning gray.

"I know Esme built it with magic," I said.

"Esme used magic to build it, yes." Harriet ran a hand over the mantle. "She also imbedded magic in every piece of it. Like the wreath on your bedroom door—the one that never dies? Magic."

The wreath wasn't the only flower arrangement that hadn't wilted, but I'd only lived in the house a few months. I guess I figured they were just well cut.

"But the magic isn't only to keep the flowers alive," Harriet said. "It's to keep you alive."

"Are you supposed to be telling me all this?" I asked. "Because Xander—"

"Is a meddler." She waved a hand around. "I know, it's annoying."

That's not what I was going to say, but the way she said it made me laugh.

She, however, still didn't break a smile.

"If the magic keeps me alive?" I asked. "Then why didn't it keep Esme alive?"

"I don't mean it protects you from illness." She looked around. "Though it might do that too," she mumbled. "But I meant it protects you from enemies."

"Is that so?" I asked. "Then how in the first few days I was here was I almost stabbed?"

"Almost." Her tone was final. "I would venture to guess the house had something to do with you not getting stabbed."

Esme's journal had saved me. But I couldn't tell her about the journal. Surely, she'd want to see it. And I was not about to share my grandmother's writings with anyone.

"Well, I'm glad the house protects me," I said as Penelope came back inside and waited for me at the bottom of the stairs. "I think that's my cue to head to bed. I have a group of ladies coming over first thing in the morning to do some exercise. You're welcome to join us if you'd like."

"I don't exercise," she said.

I shrugged, then followed Penelope up the stairs. As different as she was, the fact that she was an actual family member wiped all of that away. She couldn't be the one who killed Trinity. And if she wasn't and Melody wasn't, then who was?

"Knock, knock," Katie peeked her head in the back door the next morning. "Do I smell coffee?"

"Perfect timing," I said, pouring her a mug. "It just finished brewing."

Katie cupped the warm mug in her hands and sat on one of the stools next to the island. She closed her eyes when she took a sip, savoring the warmth.

"How was rehearsal yesterday?" I asked. "Sorry I had to leave so quickly."

"It's okay," she said. "It ended up being pretty much over, anyway. Delilah showed up, and after introductions, I sent everyone home. But today, we're going to get through the entire thing. I can feel it."

"Has the theater been cleared?"

She shook her head. "Are you still okay with using the studio? I know it's your workplace too."

"Absolutely," I said. "I'm happy to have a place for us to rehearse. We could even do the show there if it comes down to it. Though there wouldn't be much room for an audience."

"With all the snow, I don't know that we'll have much of an audience for this one." Katie wore flowing gaucho pants with a tight long-sleeved shirt I would guess was probably a bodysuit. She made my yoga pants and grey tank look so bland.

"How was Delilah?" I asked.

"She's definitely not Trinity," Katie said. "I was starting to worry Trinity would have been the better fit for Melody's role, but Delilah has no chance. I probably shouldn't have let Melody choose the runner-up, but oh well."

I sipped my coffee and considered Melody's point of view. She'd gotten passed over for one role, then almost kicked out of a role in her mother's own production. It only made sense she'd bring in someone non-threatening.

"Did Melody know you were considering giving Trinity her role?" I asked.

"I may have mentioned it," Katie said, then quickly added. "But that doesn't mean Melody hurt Trinity."

"I know," I said. "I don't think she did. But the evidence against her . . ."

"Yeah," Katie said.

We sat in silence for a few minutes, lost in thought before a knock at the door interrupted. Nancy, Fran, Amy, and Bonnie all came walking in together.

"Good morning," I said, hopping up to prepare their coffee.

"You don't have to make it," Bonnie said. "We are perfectly capable."

"That's why you pay me the big bucks." I laughed. Even though it seemed like a casual morning get together, I'd created it as an actual therapeutic session.

"What's the plan for this morning?" Amy asked, taking a drink of the coffee I'd handed her.

"I thought we'd do some stretching," I said. "Nothing too strenuous."

"That's good." Amy smiled. "Because I'm still sore from that weight lifting routine you had us do the other day."

"Me too," Fran said. "That was brutal."

"Oh, come on," Nancy said. "It wasn't that bad."

"I barely got up this morning," Bonnie said. "Between

running the hardware store, the development business, and helping with the play, I'm flat exhausted."

"You know, you don't have to help with the play," Katie said. "Not that we don't want you there—we do. It's just that the show would go on."

"I know." Bonnie smiled. "But it's been good for me to get back into the acting and production stuff. I was getting really down. Which brings me to something else."

We all looked at her in her perfect workout outfit with a ballerina bun affixed neatly to the top of her head. Even when she was tired, she looked more put together than the rest of us.

"I'd like to make things right." Bonnie pulled a manila envelope from her oversized designer purse. "With Nancy."

Nancy glanced up from her coffee, her rosy cheeks matching the rest of her outfit. "What do you mean?"

"Every day, I walk through my front door knowing it's not where I'm meant to be," Bonnie said. "Though it's the last place PJ was alive, I've come to terms with the fact that he's moved onto another dimension. His soul doesn't live in the house. And when it comes down to it, mine shouldn't either."

Nancy shifted in her seat, a hesitant smile turning the corners of her mouth upward.

"I'd like to give the property back to yours and Hank's family. It should have gone to you all along." Bonnie pulled out a stack of legal-looking papers. "I'm so sorry you lost a sister-in-law, brother-in-law, and your son ended up in jail because of it. If I'd have known, I would have told Percy—" Bonnie took a shaky breath and cleared her throat. "I would have told Percy to keep his will the way it was. Then I wouldn't have lost the two people I loved more than anything in this world."

As much as everyone tried to vilify Bonnie when she'd first arrived, she was a victim of Percy's cheating too. She thought he loved her and only her—the same as Helen had. Heck, they'd had a kid—PJ—together.

"I am so sorry Ty killed them," Nancy said. "I swear I didn't raise him like that. I think about it all the time. Where did I go wrong? How could the boy I fed and clothed and read stories to and cuddled every night have gone so far off course?"

"From what I can tell, it's not your fault," Bonnie said. "You and Hank are two of the nicest people I've ever met."

"But what about you?" I asked Bonnie, trying to keep my emotions off my face even though I knew my hair was probably a shade of blue at the moment. "Does that mean you're leaving?"

"It means we won't be neighbors anymore," Bonnie said. "But you can't get rid of me that easily. I'm going to move into the apartment over the hardware store. It's the perfect size for me."

Sniffles came from all around me.

"All right, all right, that's enough," Fran said, wiping her eyes. "That's a real nice thing of you to do, Bonnie."

Nancy opened her arms, and she and Bonnie hugged for a solid thirty seconds.

"Now," Fran said to me when they'd finished hugging, and everyone stopped crying. "What's the scoop on Trinity?"

23

I gave them the basics of the case—nothing that would jeopardize anything—before moving into our stretches. Harriet didn't join us. By the time we were finished, she had set up all her evidence on the table.

"Ooh, what's all this?" Nancy said as we finished our workout.

"I'm investigating two murders," Harriet said, not being discreet in the slightest.

"Two?" Fran poked her head in.

"My mother's and Trinity's," she said. "They both died the same way."

It was Katie's turn to come in. "I'm sorry, who are you?"

Harriet didn't look up from what she was doing. "Harriet Nightingale."

Katie looked like she might pass out, her coffee cup slipping from her hands and shattering on the floor.

This made Harriet look up. "Have we met?"

Katie shook her head, then turned and walked to the kitchen.

I didn't know how Katie hadn't heard Harriet introduce herself to Jake in the barn, but she was probably preoccupied with Trinity's death.

Harriet shrugged and went back to what she was doing.

I followed Katie, where she stood bracing herself on the island, taking deep breaths.

"Are you okay?" Fran asked, the lot of them coming up behind me.

Katie looked up at us. "That's—she's—"

"We know," Nancy moved to her side and started rubbing her back. "It's okay."

Bonnie looked confused, but now probably wasn't the best time to clue her in on the drama.

"Jake said—" Katie gasped for air. "He said it was an accident."

"Why is she here?" Fran asked me. "In your house?"

"Little did I know, I have a cousin," I said, trying to keep things light.

But at this declaration, Katie passed out.

Thankfully, Nancy was there to help. She caught Katie and lowered her to the ground.

I grabbed a towel and rolled it up to go under Katie's head like a pillow.

"I'll go take care of the mess," Bonnie said, grabbing the broom and dustpan from my cupboard.

"Thanks," I said.

When Katie regained consciousness, she looked at us in shock. "Please tell me that was all a dream?"

No one said anything.

Katie moaned and rolled onto her side, pushing herself into a seated position. "Let's rewind a bit," Katie said. "Harriet thinks she's going to find her mother's killer, and she's your cousin?"

"Half-cousin," I said. "I think. We have the same grandfather but different grandmothers."

"And you're quite certain about this?" Nancy asked.

"Jake knew too," I said. "I figured since he confirmed it, it was probably true."

Katie huffed. "Help me up."

I did, and we all stood.

"I told Esme not to mess around with Jonathan Renard," Katie said.

"Wait, Renard?" I asked. "As in Renard's Curse?"

"Who told you it was called Renard's Curse?" Katie asked, her eyes wide.

"That would be me," Amy said. "Sorry, I didn't know it was a secret."

"Is it related to this same man?" I asked. "My grandfather?"

Amy looked at Katie for permission to speak. Katie finally nodded.

"He and Veronique—Harriet's grandmother—lived in the theater together until one day she packed up and left," Amy said. "We never saw her again."

"We think he drove Veronique away when he found out the child she was carrying was a girl." Katie took a breath. "That's why the curse only targets women—one of which being the daughter he didn't want."

A shiver ran down my spine. "You think he somehow killed his own daughter because he wanted a son?"

Katie shrugged. "We didn't know any of this, though, when he set his sights on Esme."

"We all knew what he wanted," Fran said.

I glanced around. "What?"

"Another chance to spread his seed," Fran said. "He wanted a boy to carry on the Renard family name."

"And he thought Esme would be the perfect woman to help him carry that out," Amy said.

"When he left town, she swore up and down that he wasn't Emily's father," Katie said. "And I stupidly believed her."

"Did you know he was a warlock?" I asked.

Katie nodded. "The first one to come into town for years. And the last one to come into town until your Xander showed up."

My Xander.

A blush crept up my neck, and Penelope oinked beside me, alerting me to the change in my hair.

"Ooh," Amy said. "What's that all about?"

"Nothing," I said. "It's nothing."

"As cute as the two of you are, be careful," Katie said. "Warlocks have a reputation for only caring about themselves."

Her words hit a nerve. Even though Xander had been there for me at various times, he still seemed to do whatever he wanted whenever he wanted. I couldn't let myself get caught up in that kiss. The kiss was about one thing— changing my hair.

"I understand why Harriet wants to investigate her

mother's killer," Fran said, glancing at Katie to make sure she wouldn't faint again. "But why is she investigating Trinity's? She never came to town to investigate any of the other women the curse hit."

"To be fair, no one else died," Nancy said.

"I think she's investigating because she thinks whoever killed Trinity was trying to kill her," I said. "She got a note to meet someone on stage that night so they could give her information about her mother's death. Then the trapdoor opened with Trinity on stage."

"Veronique was convinced Ambeline was murdered too," Katie said. "But Jake assured her over and over again that it was a stage malfunction and that the stage had been fixed. I'd even offered to pay Veronique for pain and suffering—I knew she had a granddaughter who might need the extra financial support." Katie glanced back toward the dining room. "But she refused. She always said if she agreed to take the money, that would be like accepting a lie."

"Do you think Jonathan could have killed Ambeline?" I asked.

"If he did, he might have tried to kill Harriet too," Katie said. "And if he's trying to kill her family, that means he'll come after you next."

I held up a hand. "Harriet said he died."

Katie frowned. "When?"

"A week ago," I said. "She thinks she got the letter from another of our cousins who wants us dead. Or at least her dead. He may or may not know about me."

"How is that supposed to make me feel better?" Katie asked.

That was a fair point. "I don't think he knows about me. Maybe that's why Emily left me at a fire station." The memory of the picture popped into my head. "Oh, hold on." I ran upstairs, taking two at a time to retrieve the photo I'd carefully placed on the nightstand.

When I got back downstairs, out of breath, I handed Katie the photo. The other ladies huddled around to see it.

Their expressions matched my own feelings every time I saw my mother holding me. Their eyes teared up as they looked at me.

"If you ever had any question about whether your mom loved you," Katie said, "this picture should answer that for you."

I nodded, unable to form words.

She handed it back to me. "What are you going to do? If one of your cousins is trying to kill off both of your family lines, that means your life is in danger."

"I haven't really gotten that far yet," I said. "Harriet wanted to chat with me about it after our morning session."

"Chat away," Katie said. "We're going to go home and get ourselves cleaned up. Are you still up for rehearsal tonight?"

"I'll be there," I said.

"Good." Katie nodded. "And we're going all the way through, so you better get that line of yours figured out."

I smiled. "I'll see what I can do."

24

"I thought they'd never leave," Harriet said.

I sat opposite Harriet, looking at everything she had methodically arranged on the table. "Have you made any progress?"

"Unfortunately, no," Harriet said. "I believe I need to do something a bit out of the ordinary to catch the killer."

I looked down at the evidence on the table. "I don't understand the timeline," I said. "Your grandfather came to town, hooked up with your grandmother."

"It was more than a hook-up," Harriet said. "They were in love."

"They were together," I agreed. "Then your grand-mother left, and he and Esme—"

"Hooked up."

I shrugged. It wasn't for me to judge what my grand-mother had done.

"Then what? He left town? And when does this cousin come into the picture? Because I feel like he'd have to be much older than us to have killed your mother."

She pulled out a long blank piece of paper and set it on the table in front of me. As her finger traced over it, a timeline appeared. I'd never seen someone's magic work like this. Other than Xander's knife trick, all the magic I'd encountered had practically been accidental from my hair.

"Our grandfather sired his first child—a girl—years before he came to Cliff Haven. I haven't found much about her other than she had a son only a few years after Emily was born."

"Meaning he would have been old enough to kill your mother after she had you."

"Correct," Harriet said. "As for why he left town, I can only suppose it was because he'd already impregnated the two witches in town, both of whom would have girls." She pulled out another photograph of a man. "This was Jonathan. Go ahead, touch it."

"Why?"

"You might glean something from it," she said.

I hesitated. What could I possibly glean from touching a photograph? Sure, I'd felt all warm and fuzzy when I'd touched the one of Emily and me, but that was because it was a sweet picture, right?

"Just touch it." She shoved it closer to me.

I did and felt . . . nothing.

"You're not even trying," she said. "Pick it up. Try to feel something. We're never going to figure anything out if you don't try."

I picked up the photograph and tried to feel something. Anything. I looked at the man in front of me. Had he really sired three women only to have their children end up at odds? That's not what family was supposed to be about. Family was supposed to be there for you, not try to kill you.

"Sorry," I said, handing it back. "All I feel is disgust."

She shrugged. "At least disgust isn't nothing."

"So did he end up having any more kids after he left Cliff Haven?" I asked.

"No," she said. "Not that I can find, anyway. And I believe that has something to do with your grandmother."

"Esme?" I asked.

A conspiratorial grin came over her face. "Yes. I believe Esme made him incapable of having any additional children. And after my mother died, I believe Esme made it impossible for Jonathan or any of his heirs besides you to find Cliff Haven."

"Which is why you couldn't find Cliff Haven until he died?" I said. "And that could be why Emily hasn't come back."

"Perhaps," she said. "But now that he's dead, I could find it. Which means . . ."

"So can our cousin."

She nodded. "He may have already killed one person trying to get to me. We can't let him kill anyone else."

"How are we supposed to stop him?"

"I have an idea."

"Okay."

"He wants me," she said. "He knows I'm the one who stands in his way."

I glanced back at the timeline.

"I need to make it very clear where I'll be and when so that he'll try to kill me and then we can kill him."

"Wait," I said, looking up at her. "You want to kill him?"

"If it's between him or me, yes," Harriet said. "And I believe it is."

"Then I need to tell Jake and Xander."

"No," she said.

"What do you mean, no?" I leaned forward. "We can't do this on our own. For all we know, we'll end up the same way our mothers did." A thought dawned on me. "Do you think they were trying to set him up too?"

"If they were, good," she said. "But they probably underestimated him. We can't do the same."

"But they both had magic," I said.

"So do we."

"You might, but I don't. I mean, I do, but I don't know how to use it."

"Then you need to figure it out," she said. "Today."

I laughed. "You want me to just figure it out?"

"Why not?"

"Xander said you're not supposed to push me into using it."

"Xander, Xander, Xander," she said. "What do you even know about him? How can you be sure what he's telling you is the truth? Just because he's the first magical person you met, doesn't mean he's honest."

"He told me he wouldn't lie to me," I said.

"He told you? Oh then, certainly, believe him." Her sarcasm was cutting.

"I've known him longer than I've known you."

"But you aren't related to him," Harriet said. "Come

on. You know you want to know how to access your magic. Why wouldn't you?"

"And you can help me . . . safely?"

She shrugged. "Let's find out."

B efore I knew it, I was standing on the edge of my cornfield, trying to imagine a pond that I knew was there but couldn't see.

"Focus," Harriet said. "Look for the edges of magic, then follow it in."

I tried. I looked up and down, but nothing was working.

She rubbed her hands over her arms. The sun was rising, but the cold had momentarily stopped the snowfall. "Here, let's see if this works." She took a step into the field—which was now a big, flat, snow-covered piece of land—and spread her arms wide. "Now can you see it?"

"I don't know what I'm supposed to be seeing."

"The trees." She motioned above her. "The ice."

"What do the edges of magic look like?"

"How am I supposed to know?" Harriet asked. "I've been able to use my magic since I could remember. I never had to learn."

This sparked something inside me. "Hold on," I said. "I'll be right back."

I'd left the photo on the counter after Katie and the gang had gushed over it. When I returned to the field, Harriet was running around jumping in the air every once in a while.

"What are you doing?" I called to her.

"I'm skating," she said. "Can't you see that?"

I squinted, but she still seemed to be running through the snow. Sure, she was running more quickly than someone could normally run through such deep snow, but otherwise, it simply looked like she was trying to get some exercise.

"What'd you get?" Harriet asked, coming to a stop in front of me.

"I thought a photo from the last time I would have known I had magic—or someone else knew I had magic— might help."

"And did it?"

"I haven't looked," I said.

"We don't have all day. You have rehearsal soon."

I steadied myself and glanced down at the photo. My mother looked so serene. So in love. She looked at me as if I was the only person in her world.

But that was it.

"You're focusing your attention in the wrong place," Harriet said.

I glanced back at the photo.

Instead of looking at my mother, I focused on the baby. My white hair peeked out from beneath the cute little hat, and I was wrapped tightly in a blanket. Though I hadn't really focused on it, you could see my face.

And there it was. A speck. Like the speck I'd seen on the mural the night before . . . my heart sank.

The mural had been warning me about Trinity's death. Or Harriet's. And I'd done nothing but let it happen. I'd almost forgotten.

"What?" Harriet said. "You look like you saw a ghost."

"The night before Trinity died—before you were supposed to die—something might have warned me."

"Something magical?"

I nodded.

"And you see something like that in this photo too?"

I nodded again.

"I don't understand the problem," Harriet said.

"It was a warning," I said. "When I touched it, my hair turned the same color as yours. The same color as Trinity's wig."

"Let's not focus on the murders. Let's focus on the magic. Do whatever you have to do to get it to work."

The sparkle was still in my tiny little eye.

I was ready.

I needed to be able to use my magic. Especially if we wanted to figure out who killed Harriet's mother, Trinity, and maybe even find out where my mother was.

I rubbed a thumb over the sparkle, and it did the same thing as when I'd touched the one on the mural. A volt of electricity wound its way over my thumb, up my arm, and circled my neck before climbing into my scalp.

"What did it do to my hair?" I asked.

Harriet glanced up. "Nothing."

I laughed.

Surely it had done something to my hair. I felt the electricity—the magic—go to my scalp like before. But when I pulled a piece of hair toward my face to see, my hair was still white like normal.

"It might not be your hair that needed to change, but your sight," Harriet said.

I glanced up toward the field, and about ten feet in front of me, I saw it. The edge of magic Harriet was talking about.

"You see it, don't you?"

"I see something," I said.

"Good." She kept her voice low like she was trying to coax a small child from a hiding place. "Now hold on to that and look past it. Look further."

I did, and the trunk of a tree shimmered into view. Then another and another. My breath caught in my throat. My magic was working.

"I see the trees," I whispered. "Now what?"

"Look for the pond," she said. "It's clear as glass. You can see the fish underneath."

I didn't want to go too quickly, but it seemed like the more I saw, the more I saw, if that made any sense. Like when one tree came into view, three more did. Then the path leading up to the pond. Then the bench next to the pond. Then the pond itself.

I gasped. It was lovely. My insides warmed. Esme dug this pond for me.

When I looked over at Harriet, she was no longer

wearing boots but had on skates. "When I saw you running, you were actually skating, weren't you?"

"You saw me running?" she asked. "That would have been a sight. I don't think I ever ran, even as a child. It's not my style."

I laughed. "Can I skate too?"

She held out a pair of beautiful silver skates. "I think they're your size."

I had them on in a flash, and before I knew it, we were skating together. She was better than me at the spins and jumps, but I never fell. Never even felt off balance. And it had probably been ten years since I'd last been skating.

The air was noticeably warmer, almost as if we were in a magical bubble. Which this practically was. For the first time in several days, my mind steadied, and things became clearer.

I thought of the line I hadn't been able to say and mumbled it under my breath. I said the words without a problem. Perfect, so I just needed to be inside a magical bubble to say it.

I laughed at the thought of trying to conjure a magical bubble on the theater stage.

Which brought my mind to the stage itself. And the lever. Why would it have been cleaned off if someone magical had made the trapdoor open? It wouldn't have. I'd established that. Then there was the wig. At least one person had worn a wig exactly like Harriet's hair, possibly even two. But why?

Then a thought hit me. What if Harriet could change her hair? I mean, I couldn't control mine, but what if she could? She could have mimicked the wig that Trinity wore to make it seem like they'd been after her. To get me to believe she was innocent.

I glanced at my cousin. What if she was here simply to remove me from the lineage? She could have made up the other cousin completely.

My skates wobbled beneath me.

And if she did, she was setting me up.

She did another twist in the air as a crack sounded around me.

"What was that?" Harriet said, landing perfectly.

I couldn't tell what was going on, other than I knew I needed to get off the ice. Get away from Harriet.

"Stop," Harriet said, her normally monotone voice replaced with panic. "Whatever you're doing, stop. You're going to kill us both."

I wasn't doing anything other than trying—and failing —to get back to the trees. To solid ground. And back to my house. The house would protect me.

The cracking sound rang through the air again.

Harriet sped past me, hopping off the ice like it wasn't a problem at all.

"Come on," Harriet said. "Grab my hand."

She was on land, but I couldn't get close enough. My arms felt heavy. Everything felt heavy. "What are you doing?" I asked her, but my words came out like sludge out of a pipe.

"Ellie!" Xander appeared from the tree line. "Get off the ice."

But when I looked down, I wasn't on ice. I was in snow. Deep snow. The pond was gone.

When I looked back up at them, the trees were gone too.

The cold took over first. I couldn't move.

Snow fell around me more quickly than was natural. I was going to be buried alive.

"What did you do?" I heard Xander's voice ring out. It was far, so far away.

"I'm sorry," I tried to say, but sound wouldn't escape my lips. It was as if I was frozen.

The snow was up to my chest now.

"She wanted to learn," Harriet's voice. "I was trying to help."

They were fighting about me. About my magic.

This is why Xander said I had to find it on my own. But Harriet had pushed.

"It was fine until it wasn't," Harriet said.

"What changed?" Xander asked.

Why were they having a conversation while I was being buried alive? "Help me!" I tried to scream, but again my mouth wouldn't open. My voice wouldn't produce a sound.

"Nothing changed. We were having fun. She was happy. Happier than she's been since I met her. I could see it in her face. Her hair was shimmering."

Shimmering.

Like it had when Xander kissed me.

As the snow reached my neck, I realized I might never get to kiss him again. Not that he wanted to kiss me again. But I might never get to kiss anyone again.

"Help me get her out," Xander said.

"I'm trying, but I think she did this magically," Harriet said. "The ice cracked, and she fell in. Then it refroze around her. Instantly."

"Ellie?" I could hear Xander's plea even though the snow was over my ears. I tipped my head back, trying to keep my mouth and nose free. "Ellie, you have to do this. Harriet and I can't save you."

Panic welled inside me. I couldn't save myself. I didn't know how to use my magic.

"I know I told you not to push your magic, but if you don't right now, you might not get out."

"I've tried everything," Harriet said from somewhere I couldn't see. "Ellie, use the magic inside you. The magic you were born with. The magic passed on from your grandmother."

Xander's face appeared over mine. He smiled. "You can do this. You're strong. You've been rescuing yourself your entire life."

He was right. I was strong. I could do this.

I thought about the mural and the journal and the photograph. I carried the name of two strong women. Two powerful witches. Everything I needed was inside me.

A sparkle formed at the edge of my vision. Just over Xander's shoulder. I focused on it, then closed my eyes. I imagined myself reaching out to touch it.

A familiar sensation of electricity moved through my subconscious and down the length of my body.

The snow started to recede. When it reached my neck, it turned back to ice. Ice that had encased my entire body. But was now melting, releasing me from its grip.

"Good," Xander said, his smile one of relief. "Keep going."

I held onto that speck until I was above the ice.

The pond re-hardened into the clear skating rink it had originally been.

Xander gathered me up in his arms, embracing me with so much strength I felt like I was back in the ice.

Harriet fell to her knees beside us, tears streaking down her face. "I'm so sorry," she said. "I didn't mean for you to get hurt."

"Let's go up to the house so we can straighten everything out," Xander said. "Do you need help?" He released me from the hug and looked into my eyes.

"I think I can do it," I said. If I could get myself out of a magical ice-snow tomb, I could walk the quick jaunt to my house.

I had magic inside me, but I also had grit. And I might never have gotten that grit if my mother hadn't left me at that fire station.

Xander made hot cocoa while Harriet wrapped me in a blanket, and Penelope snuggled up next to me on the couch.

"I'll be right back," Harriet said.

Whatever my brain was going on about thinking she was bad was wrong. She had done nothing but dote on me and worry that I was okay. I needed to stop being so suspicious of everyone. Especially someone I could call family.

From the living room, I could hear Xander and Harriet whisper-arguing.

"You guys don't need to fight about me," I said. I felt fine, other than being ridiculously tired.

They both walked in.

"We're not fighting," Harriet said.

Xander handed me a mug of cocoa. "We're just discussing what went wrong. Do you think you could tell us?"

I didn't want to talk about the fact that my brain basically spun out of control, thinking Harriet had set me up to die. "I think I lost control of my magic," I said. "But when it mattered, I got it back."

Xander and Harriet exchanged a look.

"It's really okay," I said.

"She shouldn't have been pushing you to use your magic," Xander said.

I thought Harriet might refute this, but she simply stayed silent.

"It turned out okay." He stood and looked out the window toward the pond. "But if you had died . . ."

Maybe he cared about me more than I thought he did.

"She wasn't going to die," Harriet said. "If she couldn't have, the two of us could have gotten her out."

"Could we?" Xander turned to look at her. "Because I was trying, and there wasn't the slightest change."

"I was trying too," Harriet said. "But we weren't working together."

Xander nodded as if he knew what she was talking about. "I still don't know if that would have made a difference."

"Do you think my magic is faulty?" I asked, then took a sip of my cocoa.

"Your magic isn't faulty," Xander said. "It's simply new. And you don't know how to control it. Trying something like skating on a frozen pond—even a magical frozen pond—should have been a simple task, but something else happened."

They both looked at me expectantly.

"I think I need to go upstairs and rest before rehearsal," I said. "You guys stay and argue as much as you want."

Penelope followed me up the stairs.

Every part of me wanted to crawl into bed and sleep for the next few hours, but Penelope nudged the back of my leg, pushing me toward the entrance to the attic.

"Okay," I said. "But only for a few minutes. I'm so tired."

Penelope followed as I took the stairs slowly and curled up at my feet when I sat in the chair. I assumed she wanted me to open the journal and look for some sort of comforting words from Esme.

The journal warmed at my touch, much like the photograph had.

The photograph!

I had it before I went on the ice, but I couldn't remember what I'd done with it after that.

I searched my pants pockets, but it wasn't there. I had to go back out and get it before it got destroyed in the snow. When I reached to put the journal on the table, I missed, and it fell to the ground.

Penelope let out a surprised oink, scrambling to her feet.

"I left the photograph of my mother and me outside," I said, reaching for the journal.

But when I picked it up, something had fallen out.

The photograph.

"How is this—how did it—" It made no sense.

Penelope nudged my hand with her snout, trying to comfort me.

Magic.

It had gotten back here by magic.

I tucked it into the journal for safekeeping and sat back down.

Instead of lying at my feet, Penelope went to the window and looked outside.

The journal flipped easily to a page closer to the end. A blank page.

I tried to flip backward, but every time I did, it flipped itself back to the blank one.

"What am I supposed to do with this?" I said aloud. Maybe I was supposed to do what Harriet had done with the timeline paper.

I ran a finger along the page, but nothing appeared. "Okay, I don't know what I'm supposed to do, but I'm exhausted."

I was about to put the journal on the stand when Penelope trotted over with something in her mouth.

A pen.

"You want me to write in the journal?" I asked, taking the pen. "Where did you find this?"

She didn't respond—not that I expected her to since she was a pig—but instead, she went back to the window, leaving me with my thoughts.

The pen was heavy in my hand. But not a burdensome heavy. A comforting heavy. The kind you got from a weighted blanket or snuggles from a wiggly pink friend.

Without thinking about what I was going to write, I wrote. I wrote about how I'd come to Cliff Haven, what life was like before, Trinity's death, and how I'd encountered a magical conundrum on the ice. As I wrote, a weight seemed to lift from my shoulders.

Was this why Esme kept a journal?

My words flowed from my mind to the pen and onto the page. When I was finished, I simply closed the journal and returned it to the table.

"I think it's time to get some rest now," I said, gathering Penelope in my arms before looking out at the pond. The pond I could now see. The pond that had tried to swallow me whole.

My alarm sounded. Every part of me wanted to turn it off and sleep all the way through the night. But Katie was counting on me.

I took a shower to wake myself up before heading downstairs.

The house was silent besides my footsteps. I peeked into the dining room where Harriet sat examining all of her evidence.

For a moment, I felt bad for her. How hard would it be to live in fear for your life? To be all-consumed with finding someone who killed your mother?

"Are you going to stand there watching me, or are you going to say hi?" Harriet said without turning around.

I laughed to myself. "Hi."

"Feeling better?" She turned in her seat and examined me from head to toe. "You look okay."

"I'm better," I said. "I don't know that I was ever feeling bad. Just tired."

"And almost dead."

I shrugged. "It was scary, sure, but I don't think I was going to die. I think my magic needed to be tested."

"If that's what you want to tell yourself," she said.

"Where's Xander?" I asked, trying to keep my voice neutral.

"What is going on with the two of you?"

"Nothing," I said too quickly.

She pushed her glasses up on her nose. "Is that so?"

"Why would you think there's something going on?"

"I won't justify such an idiotic question with an answer." She turned back to the table. "Xander had to leave."

Disappointment settled in my chest. Why would he just leave?

"Made any progress on the case?" I finally asked, coming to stand next to her.

"No," she said, exasperation in her words. "It is possible that whoever lured me to Cliff Haven is gone, meaning my next move is to leave as well."

"What about our plan?"

She looked at me from the corner of her eye. "*Our* plan?"

"Your plan," I corrected. "The one about flushing the guy out? I mean, there's still a possibility that he's here."

"I don't think it's a good idea anymore." She didn't look up at me when she said this.

"Because I can't control my magic?"

She didn't respond.

"What other option do you have?"

"I can do it alone." Harriet squared her shoulders. "I have been doing it alone for many years now."

"But you don't have to now." I couldn't let her put herself in danger. She was my cousin. My only blood relative. "I may not be able to control my magic, but I'm smart in other ways."

Harriet was silent.

"Please, let me help," I said. "I don't want to see you get hurt."

Harriet looked up at me. "Don't you have a rehearsal to get to?"

I didn't feel great about leaving her alone. "Promise you won't go after him yet." I paused. "And don't leave, okay?"

"If there's one thing you and I have in common, Ellie Vanderwick, is that we don't take kindly to being told what to do. We're both perfectly capable of living life as we wish—alone."

"But now we have each other," I said. "We don't have to live life on our own. Regardless of how capable we are."

She didn't respond, but I thought I saw a small smile form on her lips. Or maybe that was what I wanted to see.

Katie and Melody were already in the barn setting up when I walked in.

"Ready to say your line today?" Katie asked.

Melody glanced up at me expectantly.

"Sure am," I lied. I hadn't practiced and wasn't sure I could do anything after the morning I had. But I had to try my best. I rolled the words over my tongue under my breath.

"You got this," Katie said, then headed to the doors to greet Nancy and Bonnie as they walked in.

"Any update on the case?" Melody said when Katie was out of earshot.

"Nothing from Jake," I said.

"I did some digging on who all was up for the role." She reached into her bag and pulled out a small sheet of paper. "These women would all have motive too, but I put a star next to the ones who actually had a shot at getting the role."

I glanced over at the list. Some of the names I'd vaguely heard of, but one stood out. Delilah. "Delilah was up for the role?"

"She auditioned." Melody shrugged. "But there was no way she was going to get it."

I noticed she hadn't starred Delilah's name.

"But she got the understudy role," I said. "Must mean she's not terrible."

A rosy blush overtook Melody's cheeks.

"Be honest," I said. "Did you give her the part because you didn't want any competition for the role after Trinity?"

"I know it looks that way," Melody said, then looked around to make sure no one was listening. "I didn't want to say anything because I didn't want Mom to know, but Trinity and Delilah are the only two who wanted the understudy. I called all the others before Delilah, but no one else wanted to spend their holiday break in the tiniest town in Iowa with a washed-up Hollywood actress."

"You're not washed up," I said, but she stopped me.

"Trinity and Delilah were friends," Melody continued.

"So, they figured they'd both come out for the holiday and spend it here for the play. It worked out that Delilah was already in town."

"Now that Trinity is gone," I said. "Who gets the role you were up for?"

"We haven't heard yet," Melody said. "But it won't be me. I already told you that."

I looked at the list in front of me. Could these people be in danger too?

"It could go to anyone on that list." She shrugged. "Well, almost anyone."

As if on cue, a tall woman walked through the door. Her eyes red as if she had been crying.

I wanted to see if she was okay, but Katie walked in and clapped her hands together. "Let's get started."

"I see you've met Delilah," Bex said, coming up behind me.

"I met her last night," I said. "She was with Dylan."

"Yuck."

"Yeah."

"How's Xander?" She wiggled her eyebrows at me.

"Xander is fine."

"No more kissing, I presume?"

"Nope."

"That's too bad."

"You're telling me," I said. We both laughed. "I did use my magic today, though. On purpose."

"Ooh," she said. "How did that go?"

"I got stuck in some ice, but I got myself unstuck too."

Bex's eyes widened. "You got stuck in ice? Were you over in the park?"

There was a state park nearby with cliffs, a few ponds, and some caves. I hadn't been there yet, but everyone said it was beautiful.

I glanced around to see if anyone was listening. "There's a magical pond behind the barn."

Bex stared at me for a minute before she burst out laughing.

"I'm serious," I said, though I could understand why she was skeptical.

"You're telling me that in your cornfield is a magical pond. And no one has fallen in? How does that even work with the harvesting?"

"It's magic."

Bex doubled over in laughter again.

"Let's get started," Katie said.

Bex was still laughing.

"Shhh," I said.

Katie gave us a warning look.

Bex stopped laughing, then looked at me and shook her head with a smile.

She didn't have to believe me.

"We're going to go through the entire play," Katie said. "This is our last run-through before we have our dress rehearsals. The police have cleared the theater, so starting tomorrow, we'll be back there."

Delilah sniffled loudly from across the room. I couldn't imagine rehearsing where my best friend had died. But it was slightly strange that she wasn't this upset last night. Maybe something had happened between then and now.

"Our first performance is this weekend," Katie said. "If the snow lets up, we'll have a packed house."

"It might be full even with the snow," Melody said. "If the roads open, there will be quite a bit of publicity surrounding Trinity's death."

"All the more reason we need to practice," Katie said. "Let's get started."

The play was an original written by Katie about a traditional family Christmas with some humor and some drama. Melody was the lead while Bex and some of the other women played her sisters.

Delilah sat off to the side, watching Melody's every move. She even took notes occasionally.

Sometimes I wondered if Katie had written the final line specifically for me.

The line I couldn't say.

The line that was quickly approaching.

I knew it. I'd practiced it in my head. I'd even said it aloud on the ice.

But as I stood to the side of the makeshift stage, watching them wrap up the play, I felt the familiar sensation of panic welling up inside me.

Part of me wanted to use my magic, but I knew I'd exhausted it on the ice. Even if I knew how, my hair was too tired to change. My magic was spent.

If only I'd known that as a kid. I could have expelled my magic in private, and my hair would have behaved. I could have stayed with a family. Maybe the one I was with when I turned sixteen. They were pretty wonderful.

Now, my only family member was inside my house. At least, that's where I thought she was.

"Ellie?" Katie whispered.

I glanced up and realized it was my turn. Everyone was

staring at me. Their faces trained in smiles, but their eyes full of frustration.

"Say your line," Melody hissed.

I sucked in a breath. "And around looking—no, sorry." I tried to remember. "And looking around—"

The door creaked open, saving me from myself.

"I'm sorry to burst in like this," Jake said, his face set in a frown.

I thought I heard Katie mumble, "Not again," under her breath.

"I have something I need to tell everyone," Jake said. "You might want to sit down."

The entire studio hushed.

"We can handle it," Katie said.

"Dylan has been in a car accident," Jake said.

"Oh my goodness," Nancy said. "Is he okay?"

I glanced over to see Melody hanging onto Jake's every word. As was Delilah.

"He's being flown to the nearest hospital." Jake pulled off his beanie. "They're not sure he'll make it."

"How did this happen?" Katie asked.

"We're not sure right now," Jake said. "But I do need to speak with Delilah and Melody, please."

"Why?" Delilah asked, her voice shaky.

"You both knew Dylan," Jake said. "I'd like to see if I can clear up a couple of things about the accident."

"Dylan was a good driver," Melody said. "He grew up here. He knew how to drive in the snow."

"Yes, I know," Jake said. "Do you mind if we talk about it more in the house?"

Delilah and Melody both froze.

"That's fine with me," I said. "Harriet might be at the table, but the living room is open. Or if you need more privacy, you can use one of the bedrooms upstairs."

"Why don't you come with us," Jake asked me. "As long as you don't need her here?"

Katie shook her head, then said to me. "Work on that line."

I nodded, then hurried off after Jake, Melody, and Delilah.

Relief filled me to find Harriet still hunched over the table, looking through stacks of paperwork and rear-ranging photographs. Part of me thought she'd take off, and I'd never hear from her again.

We sat on the couches in the living room. "Do you think we did something?" Delilah asked. "Was there something wrong with Dylan's car?"

I thought about the night we'd seen Melody lurking in the shadows.

"Not that we can tell," Jake said. "But it's not out of the question. When was the last time either of you saw Dylan?"

Neither of them spoke.

Jake waited.

I was the only one who seemed to be uncomfortable with the silence. I shifted in my seat and tried to find something interesting to look at through the window.

"Let me reword the question," Jake said. "Did either of you see Dylan today?"

Again, silence.

Delilah snuck a peek at Melody, who sat staring at her hands in her lap.

"Come on, ladies," Jake said. "We're simply trying to figure out a timeline of events."

"I was with him this morning," they both said at the same time.

Then they both glared at each other.

I looked at Jake, who didn't seem at all surprised by this.

"When did you see him?" Melody asked Delilah.

"We had breakfast at the B&B," Delilah said. "After we woke up. Together."

Melody's face paled.

Jake cleared his throat. "And when did you see him, Melody?"

"We had brunch," Melody said. "At the café. He told me he wanted to get back together. That he was done with all the other women."

"And then what happened?" Jake asked.

"He said he was leaving town," Melody said. "But he wanted to see me again. He said he would even move to Hollywood if that's what I wanted."

"He said he was going to get back with you?" Delilah laughed. "How stupid is he? After you killed his girlfriend too."

"I didn't kill anyone," Melody said through gritted teeth.

"Did either of you see him after brunch?" Jake asked.

They both shook their heads.

"Where did you find his car?" I asked. "Did it seem like he was heading out of town?"

Jake glanced at me. "We can talk about it later."

Melody narrowed her eyes at him. "Where did you find it, Jake?"

It caught me off guard how she addressed him so casually.

"Let's just say he wasn't heading out of town," Jake said.

"He was going to see that woman who works at the B&B, wasn't he?" Delilah asked with a laugh.

"What woman?" Melody said.

"You wouldn't know her," Jake said. "She's new to town." Jake turned to Delilah. "And yes, it looks like he was going to visit her, but with the snow and some faulty brakes, we found him upside down in a ditch."

Melody and Delilah both gasped. Whether it was because he was upside down in a ditch or because he had planned on seeing another woman wasn't clear.

"Did you talk to her?" I asked Jake.

"She didn't know he was coming," Jake said. "In fact, she seemed rather happy he hadn't shown up. Probably because her boyfriend was at the house."

If my hair wasn't too tired to change, it would have. This was way more drama than I was used to.

"You said faulty brakes," I said. "Do you think they were tampered with?"

Jake shrugged. "We're not certain yet."

"She grew up on a farm," Delilah said, pointing at Melody. "She probably knows exactly how to cut brake lines, or whatever."

"Just because I grew up on a farm doesn't mean I messed with the equipment," Melody said, not meeting Jake's eye.

"I'm not here to accuse anyone of anything," Jake said. "This was simply an information-gathering mission."

"Can I go see him?" Melody asked.

"Why would you want to?" Delilah said. "He was heading out to see another woman after he made all those promises to you. After he made promises to me. You found out and cut his brake lines."

Melody narrowed her eyes. "How dare you accuse me of killing not one but two people?"

"I'm not accusing anyone," Jake said. "But I do have warrants to search both of your vehicles."

"Our vehicles?" Delilah asked. "Why?"

"Because the two of you are people of interest in both cases," Jake said.

"Both cases?" Delilah asked. "But I wasn't even in town when Trinity died. Plus, she was my best friend."

"More like frenemy," Melody corrected.

"You have no clue what you're talking about." Delilah looked down at her long fake nails. "Feel free to search my car. I have nothing to hide."

Melody stood. "Well, neither do I. Search my car first."

Jake stood and followed Melody and Delilah outside.

"They're making an awfully big fuss about this case when you and I both know it wasn't either of those women who killed Trinity," Harriet said from the doorway behind me.

"Speaking of," I said, turning to her. "What are we going to do about that?"

"I have a plan." She looked past me out the window. "Do you think your magic will work if it needs to?"

I nodded. "I know it will." It had to. I didn't have any choice.

"Good," she said, still not looking at me. "But first, you're probably going to want to see what's going on out there."

I turned to see Jake putting Melody in handcuffs.

Katie walked out of the barn with a big smile on her face at the same time I walked out the back door.

When she saw what was happening, her face fell. "What are you doing, Jake?"

"Melody is under arrest," Jake said, easing Melody into the back seat of his police car.

"I don't know how those got in there," Melody said, her voice pleading. "They're not mine. I swear. I didn't do anything to Dylan's car. I didn't hurt anyone."

"You killed her." Delilah was hysterical—screaming and throwing her hands around. "And you tried to kill Dylan too."

I hurried to Jake's side. "What did you find?"

"We found a pair of side cutters inside a rag covered in what I'm guessing will be brake fluid when we get tested," Jake said.

"No," Katie said. "You've made a mistake. Melody wouldn't hurt anyone."

"We're going to get this all sorted out," Jake said.

Katie glanced at Melody, who was crying in the back of the police car. "Can I tell her something quickly before you leave?"

"Miss Katie, I—"

"Jacob Mulroney, I've known you since you were still peeing in your pants."

Jake's face reddened. "Be quick." He opened the back door.

"You got the role," Katie said, showing Melody her phone. "The story just broke."

Melody smiled slightly. "Now, I have to prove my innocence."

Katie's phone pinged, and Melody's face fell.

"How do they know already?" Melody asked.

Katie glanced at her phone, her eyes widening. Then she glanced up at Jake. "How does the news already know Melody's been arrested?"

She looked around at the cast members who had come outside to see what the commotion was. "Which of you leaked it to the press?"

No one responded.

"It was Delilah," Melody said from the car.

Delilah raised her hands in defense. "I don't even have my phone on me. It's in my car." She turned to Jake. "Speaking of, do you still need to check it, or can I head to the hospital?"

"I'll give it a once over," Jake said, closing Melody's door.

He walked over to Delilah's car, where she pulled out her phone and waved it around for the crowd to see. "See? There's no way I could have sent it to the media."

I opened my phone to the news app to find a photo of Trinity and Dylan walking into Belinda's B&B together was under the headline.

Jealous Ex-Starlet Suspected of Murder and Attempted Murder

W hen the driveway cleared, leaving Penelope and me alone, she and I sat on the bench next to the pond so I could try to collect my thoughts. Unfortunately, they weren't cooperating.

"What's going on, Penelope?" I asked.

Everything seemed so crazy. Melody may or may not have killed and tried to kill two people.

I had a cousin who I never knew about who thought someone was trying to kill her.

Another cousin existed who would want me dead if he knew I was alive.

Also, my mother was part of it somehow. And every time I tried to get a handle on any bit of information, my mind slipped back to that photo. The one that had spurred my magical abilities. The one I was going to frame. The one that broke my heart every time I saw it.

"El, you okay?" Xander's voice broke through the silence as he walked through the trees.

I felt the hot tears make paths down my face. I hugged

my knees up into my chest and squeezed. "Everything is so messed up."

"Jake called," Xander said, sitting on the bench next to Penelope. "He said you might need some support with everything going on. I tried to call, but your phone kept going to voicemail."

"I turned it off when it started blowing up about the whole Melody murder thing."

Penelope curled up next to Xander's leg.

"Do you think she did it?" he asked.

"No, but she had every opportunity to," I said. "She was at the theater when it happened and was in the alley before Dylan's car got towed. She could have messed with his brakes. She probably didn't think she'd kill them, but still."

"It sounds like you think she might have done it."

"I don't know. I don't want to think she did. Especially because Harriet's version of the story gets me closer to answers about my mom."

Xander inhaled and then started coughing like he was choking on his own spit.

"You okay?" I asked, wiping the tears from my face.

His face was turning red, but he was still coughing, which meant he wasn't choking. Penelope looked up at him as if he was a serious imposition on her sleep.

I laid a hand on his arm. Instantly, his coughing subsided.

"How did you do that?" he asked.

"Ask Harriet," I said. "Apparently, I have healing abilities."

Xander looked at me as if this was no surprise at all. "Tell me what she said about your mom."

He wasn't usually so firm in his tone. "Uh, well, she said that her mom and my mom were sisters—half-sisters, I suppose—and that they have another half-sister who had a son around the time Emily was born. And that man is trying to kill everyone in our family lines so he can have all the superpowers of our grandfather who died last week."

Xander took a deep breath and ran a hand through his hair. "Is that all?"

"She also showed me a photo of my mom and me when I was born." I started tearing up again. "She looked so happy. I don't understand why . . ." I didn't finish the sentence. I couldn't. It hurt too much.

"So she told you your mom died?"

"No, but my mom was apparently there when her mom died. She found a bracelet under the stage. I found one of the charms when we were down there, remember?"

Xander nodded.

"Well, she had the other pieces." I looked down at Penelope, who had returned to her slumber at Xander's feet. "I guess Jake gave it to my mother."

"Is that all she said?"

I tried to think about all the things she might have said, but I couldn't come up with anything else. "That's all."

"So she's trying to rope you into helping with this investigation because she wants you to think it'll help you find your mom?"

"You and Jake should hang out," I said. "The two of you think the same way."

Xander sighed. "From what I know of Harriet and her family, they're not as upstanding as she probably claims to be."

"She may not be what she seems," I said, standing. "But she's still my family. Or are you going to tell me that's not true either?"

"No, that's true," he said, looking up at me.

I narrowed my eyes. "What else do you know about me that I don't?"

"Nothing . . . that I can share." There was the honesty I was so used to.

"Why? Why can't you share it?"

"Because it's not my place." Xander stood.

"Maybe it *is* your place. You're my friend, right? Friends don't keep secrets from each other."

Xander laughed. "That's not true at all. Friends keep secrets all the time. You keep secrets from me too."

"How do you know?"

"Well, how would I? They're secrets." He shrugged. "But I'm sure you have some."

He was probably right, but I wouldn't give him the satisfaction. "You know, it's not fair that you won't tell me anything about yourself. How are we supposed to be friends when you know everything about me, and I know nothing about you?"

"You're the one who keeps calling us friends." I could tell he regretted the words the minute they came out of his mouth.

That didn't make them hurt any less. "I think you

should go. I'm fine. If Harriet was going to kill me, she would have done it already."

Xander didn't say anything for a few seconds, then said, "I'm sorry, El. You know we're friends. I'm not good at sharing, that's all."

Part of me wanted to use this vulnerability to get him to tell me something about himself, but the other part of me wanted him to leave. I already felt stupid, assuming we were friends. How stupid would I feel if he knew how much I actually liked him?

"It's okay," I said. "We don't have to be friends. I have other friends." I motioned toward the driveway. "I'll see you around."

He took the hint and walked past me. "I really am sorry."

30

Katie thought it would be a good idea for the entire cast to meet for breakfast the next day before heading to the theater together.

I sat between Delilah and Bex as Katie made a speech about how the show must go on. Though she tried to keep a cheerful face, she spoke through tears.

It had to be hard knowing your daughter was locked up for a crime she didn't commit. And even harder wondering if, perhaps, she had.

But it was highly unlikely that both Nancy and Katie's children were murderers. If they were, it would be the perfect time for me to look at leaving Cliff Haven.

When Katie's speech finished, the two Charlies and another waitress brought us our food.

I, of course, had the crispy-edged pancakes while most of the cast, including Bex and Delilah, had boring meals of egg whites and toast. At least Bex put butter and jelly on her toast.

As I was digging into my pancakes, Delilah's phone rang.

"Hello?" she said. "No, not the black one. The brown one."

She paused, and I made eye contact with Katie, who sat across from me. I shrugged.

"That's unacceptable," Delilah said. "Fix it, or you're fired." She jabbed at the end button on the screen and shoved her phone back into her designer purse. "Assistants are so stupid sometimes. I can't seem to find a good one. This one has only been with me a couple of days, and she's already messing things up." She glanced at Katie. "Does Melody have a good assistant?"

Katie smiled, though I could tell it was fake. "Melody doesn't need one when she's not working. She does her own errands."

"Seems like a silly waste of time when you have the money to spare," Delilah said, sipping her coffee.

I wanted to ask Delilah why she needed an assistant at all. And how she paid for it but decided against it. It would be rather rude to ask.

"I'd like to pay for the entire cast's meal today." Delilah pulled a wad of cash from her purse and tried to hand Katie two hundred-dollar bills. "That should do it, right?"

Katie's eyes widened. "Absolutely not." Katie shoved the money back at Delilah. "The food is on the house." She stood and addressed everyone. "Eat up. Rehearsal starts in two hours, and we still have to get our makeup and costumes on." She abandoned her food. "I'll meet you over there."

Before walking out the door, she whispered something to the waitress. Probably about her paying for the food.

"You shouldn't have done that," Bex said, leaning forward to look at Delilah.

"Why not?" Delilah said. "I was just trying to be nice."

Something in Delilah's tone said she wasn't simply trying to be nice, but I was probably overthinking it.

I tried to enjoy my pancakes, but they couldn't stand up to the death glares everyone kept throwing at Delilah.

"Did you go see Dylan?" I asked.

"He's in a coma." She shrugged, then leaned closer to me. "I can't believe Melody would try to kill him."

"Do you really think she did?" I asked.

"The police found the cut brake lines." She shrugged. "I'd say the evidence is pretty damning."

Why hadn't I heard this? I pulled out my phone to see if Jake had texted me but found nothing.

"So, do you think you're up to following in Melody's footsteps?" Bex asked Delilah, leaning forward. "Or Trinity's, for that matter?"

"I'll never be as good as Trinity was," Delilah said, choking up a bit. "She would have taken Hollywood by storm." Delilah took one last sip of coffee, wiped away the tears forming in her eyes, and stood. "I need to get ready." She stormed out of the restaurant.

The group of us finished our food and walked together to the theater. Snow was still falling, but accumulation seemed to have slowed.

When we walked into the lobby, my hair buzzed. Something was going on. Or it could have been the after-effect of Trinity's murder. Either way, it put me on edge.

Katie had hired a few hair and makeup artists from the city to get us ready, but with the snow, they'd all canceled. Which didn't seem like the biggest deal in the world to me, but when we walked into the dressing room, Delilah was raging.

"She said we have to do our own hair," she yelled into the phone. "Can you believe that?"

We all stopped to listen.

"No, I don't need another pair. I need you to get your skinny butt down here and do my hair." She paused. "What do you mean you don't do hair? You're my personal assistant. You do whatever I tell you to do. And while you're at it, bring my makeup. You'll have to do that too."

She jabbed the disconnect button before they would have been able to answer.

"Don't get any ideas," Delilah said, pointing at us. "She's *my* assistant. If you want someone to do your hair and makeup, get your own."

"I don't think that will be necessary, dear," Nancy said, walking in with a cheery smile on her face. She wore a long red velvet dress with shiny red shoes. With it being so close to Christmas, it was a wonder children didn't stop her on the streets thinking she was Mrs. Claus. "I've completed cosmetology school. My business is Nancy's Nails, but I do all the things."

Delilah looked at her in disgust. "I'm fine waiting for my assistant, thanks."

Nancy seemed unconcerned about Delilah's brush-off.

"Well, I will definitely need help," I said, stepping forward.

The rest of the group came forward too.

"Let's get this show on the road then," Nancy said.

As she worked on each of our hair—some women doing their own or each other's making the process go more quickly—Fran brought out the costumes.

Oohs and ahhs sounded through the dressing room— which had been put back together—as she handed each of us a custom costume. Mine was gold with tiny mirrors to reflect the light.

"I can make adjustments if needed," Fran said. "But you'll have to tell me today. There won't be any adjustments made the day of the show."

My heart quickened. The show was tomorrow. And I still hadn't said my line.

"This will never fit me," Delilah squealed from her chair. Her assistant still hadn't shown up to do her hair or makeup.

"Don't worry," Fran said. "I'll make the final changes tonight."

Delilah pulled on the dress to find that it was slightly too tight and far too short. Everyone watched as she sucked in and tried to zip the zipper.

"Don't force it, or you won't have a costume at all," Fran said.

"I can't practice like this," Delilah said. "The entire back is open."

Fran thought about this for a moment, then grabbed

another garment off the rack. It wasn't as pretty as the one Delilah had on, but it wasn't terrible either.

"Use this one today," Fran said. "They're about the same shape, but this one is slightly bigger."

Delilah put on the other dress and glanced in the mirror. The shape was similar, but that was all that was. The color was an ugly green, the neckline was so high it nearly reached Delilah's chin, and the sleeves went way past her fingertips.

"This is horrible," Delilah said.

Fran shrugged. "It's all we have for today," she said. "But I assure you, I'll have this one all fixed up before the performance."

Delilah rolled up her sleeves, and I thought I saw her wince in pain, but I couldn't tell what hurt. Maybe the sleeves were too tight around her arms.

"It's about time you showed up," Delilah yelled, her gaze on the doorway.

A tiny woman probably in her mid-forties had walked in juggling several shopping bags.

"Here, I can help," I said, rushing over to grab a couple of the bags.

"She can do it herself," Delilah said. "That's why I pay her the big bucks."

"I'm Ellie," I said.

"Linda," the assistant said in a hushed voice. "Thanks for your help."

I dropped the bags at Delilah's feet. "You should be nicer," I said. "Linda is here to help you after all."

Delilah looked at me with a bit of confusion, then said, "She practically begged me to hire her. And I *pay* her to help me. It's not like she's doing this out of the kindness of her heart." She snatched the bags up off the floor. "Did you get everything right this time?"

"I think so," Linda said, her voice full of fear.

I couldn't believe we were stuck with such a monster as our lead. I needed to help Harriet find the man who actually killed Trinity so Melody could come back and take her rightful place in the production.

But that would have to wait until after rehearsal. Harriet said she'd get everything set up and fill me in with all the details tonight. It took everything in me not to worry about what she had planned and focus on the task at hand—saying my line.

Once we were all dressed and ready to go, Katie stepped into the dressing room and said, "You look wonderful. I am so thankful to have a fantastic cast for this production. It's been a pleasure in my life to create stories I love and see them acted out on stage. Today will be a fun—but important—day. Pretend like there's a crowd." She looked at me. "Get your lines right. Tomorrow, it's for real."

I could do this. I couldn't let Katie down.

But when the play sped toward my moment, I could feel the dread building inside me. I took deep breaths, rolled my wrists, and smiled. Not only had I never actually executed the line, but I was also suspended above the entire stage looking down.

I was the star. Literally. The tiny mirrors shone from my dress, casting little sparkles all around the theater. If only they were magical sparkles. I could grab onto one and use it to calm my nerves enough to say my line.

Delilah—who had not only memorized her lines perfectly but also executed them almost as well as Melody—was on her last monologue. Soon, she would exit the stage, leaving me to conclude the play.

It was a simple line. Nothing too dramatic. But it encompassed so much. Maybe it was the actual words themselves I had a hard time saying. I wasn't an actress, and pretending wasn't my forte. Or maybe it was the stage fright.

I could see Katie's gaze flitting between Delilah and me. When she landed on me, I smiled. I could do this. I had to do this.

Just as Delilah was finishing her line, the doors from the lobby burst open, and people streamed in, all holding cameras.

31

I thought Katie might kill someone when Delilah jumped off the stage and began answering the reporter's questions about Trinity and Melody.

"That's enough," Katie yelled. "Everyone out."

But they didn't listen to her. Not a single one budged.

In fact, one came toward her and said, "You're the owner and Melody's mother, correct?"

Katie promptly held her hand up to the camera lens, blocking its view.

Within seconds, Nancy, Bonnie, Fran, and Amy had joined forces with Katie, and they began moving the reporters back up the auditorium aisles toward the lobby doors.

Once the doors were closed, Katie turned back to me. "Ellie, I need you to say your line. One time."

I was still suspended in the air. I took a breath and said, "And looking around at all our family . . ." But I couldn't finish. My throat constricted.

"Keep going," Katie said.

I tried, but it was no use. Tears welled in my eyes.

"That's enough," Delilah said. "Her line doesn't matter one bit. I need to be in front of those cameras."

The rest of the cast was silent.

"You can go," Katie said. "As we say, the show must go on."

"Oh, come off it," Delilah said. "You think you're all big time because your daughter—a *murderer*—used to be famous?"

I flinched with every word Delilah said.

Bonnie walked back down the aisle toward where Delilah looked like she might tackle Katie.

"That is enough," Bonnie said. "I told Melody to do this to Trinity, but it seems she didn't get the chance."

Delilah stood a bit taller. "What are you going to do? Murder me?"

Bonnie handed Delilah a folded piece of paper.

Delilah looked stunned.

"Go ahead, open it." Bonnie smiled.

Delilah did, her face paling. "You can't do this. You're not in charge." Delilah looked at Katie. "She's putting me on probation."

"Didn't you know?" Katie said sweetly. "Bonnie is the casting director. She can do whatever she pleases when it comes to the cast."

Bonnie nodded. "As the note states, this is a warning. If you choose to continue treating the people around you unprofessionally and disrespectfully, you will be let go from the production."

"You can't let me go," Delilah said. "I'm your only option. Everyone else is either dead or in jail."

"There are alternatives," Katie said.

"You're bluffing," Delilah said, then turned to Linda. "She's bluffing. They can't fire me. I'm not even a paid actress." She crumpled up the note and threw it across the room.

"You may want to choose your actions wisely," Bonnie said. "There will be acting scouts at the performance. Katie may not have become an actress herself, but she is rather—as you call it—*big time* when it comes to Holly-wood circles."

Katie smiled through the tears pooling in her eyes.

"I'd suggest you deal with whatever grief you're feeling right now over the death of your friends and come back tomorrow ready to act your butt off," Bonnie said.

Delilah looked like she wanted to say something else but thought better of it.

Instead, she marched back up toward the auditorium exit doors, grabbing Linda by the arm on her way.

"Ouch," Linda said. "That hurts."

Delilah dropped her arm and slammed open the doors. The reporters were no longer on the other side.

Bonnie and Katie talked in low whispers as Bex lowered me down from my elevated position.

"You might be in luck. We might not be having a play after all," Bex said. "If they don't have a lead, we're done."

"We have to have the play," I said. "Even if I can't say the last line, the play has to happen."

I thought of Harriet's plan. It had to work. With every-thing going on, Katie's reputation would be ruined without this play.

I changed out of my dress, carefully hanging it on the rack, and put on a pair of black leggings and a black sweatshirt.

"A bunch of us are going out tonight," Bex said. She still had on her stage makeup but had changed into a pair of jeans and a hoodie. "Are you coming?"

"I have . . . plans."

Her eyes widened. "With Xander?" She looked me up and down. "I hope you're going to change. Unless you're going for some kind of goth look."

My chest tightened at the sound of Xander's name. "Xander and I had a bit of a falling out."

"A falling out or a lover's quarrel?"

I laughed. Bex always knew how to cheer me up. "Either way, it wasn't fun."

"At least you have someone to quarrel with," she said. "Maybe tonight I'll find my Xander."

"Good luck," I said.

"You sure you don't want to come?"

"I'm sure," I said. "Next time?"

"Deal."

Bex walked away to meet up with her friends. A month ago, I would have been happy to decline an invitation to go out, but tonight I was sad I couldn't go. I had a good reason, but still.

I pulled out my phone and dialed Harriet's number.

"Ready?" she said without even saying hello.

"I'm ready," I said.

The snow had stopped falling, but the wind blew with a ferocity I'd never seen.

Harriet had put something out to the magical world that she'd be in the town square waiting for information about her mother's death.

"Do you have on the wig?" Harriet asked.

"The wig, black hat, and black clothes."

"Good," she said. "Now, all you have to do is go to the bench and sit there. Other than for the alert, don't use your magic. I'll make sure nothing happens to you."

"And if this person actually wants to talk to you about your mother, I'll take all that information down."

"We've discussed the likelihood of that being minimal."

We'd gone through this at length, mainly when I was trying to talk her out of killing our cousin.

"Remember, if you kill someone, you'll go jail. You'll be the prime suspect in Trinity's murder and maybe even Dylan's attempted murder."

She didn't respond.

"Anyway, I think I have it figured out," I said. "No killing anyone."

"No promises," she said and disconnected the line.

I shoved my phone back into my satchel and walked into the park in the middle of the square.

The bench I was supposed to sit on had a magical barrier around it. When I sat, I could see the edges of the magic. But if I could, wouldn't someone else with magic be able to see it too? Or did that matter? Did they expect Harriet to place protections around herself?

I waited for the signal that Harriet was in place.

Finally, after what seemed like forever, my phone rang once, and then the caller hung up. When I glanced at the screen, it was Harriet's number.

She was in position. Now, all I had to do was make myself known.

I did exactly as Harriet instructed. I searched for the edges of the magic and concentrated on sending out an alert. I closed my eyes and saw a speck. I imagined touching it like I had on the ice. When I did, I concentrated on the words Harriet wanted me to say.

I tried to mumble them under my breath like she'd shown me, but I only got out the first part. "I'm here to learn about my moth—"

I was supposed to say my mother's death. But I couldn't. It was just like the last line of the play. The words wouldn't come out of my mouth.

The speck of magic was slipping away. I had to do this. For Harriet. For my family. "I'm here to learn about my mother's de—"

Tears filled my eyes. I couldn't say it. Because what I was saying wasn't true. It couldn't be. I had to hold onto hope that my mother was alive. Even though I was talking about Harriet's mother, it all came down to acting. Something I couldn't do.

I took a breath and improvised. "I'm here to learn about Ambeline Nightingale's death."

When I opened my eyes, I expected to see something change.

Anything.

But the air was still cold. The stars still glowed in the sky. And the park was still empty.

I looked around me, trying not to seem too anxious.

That's when I saw it.

Someone was walking toward me. A shadow of a person.

And in his hand was something that reflected the moonlight. Something sharp.

A knife.

3 2

I sucked in a breath. Harriet had me covered. I couldn't freak out.

The shadow walked closer, not even trying to hide the knife.

A thought crossed my mind. Could witches and warlocks not kill each other with their magic? Why had he killed Trinity with the trapdoor? And why was he coming at me with a knife?

He was only a few paces from me when another shadow came up behind him.

Was it Harriet?

I shifted on the bench. I was supposed to be a tough witch. I was supposed to be Harriet.

But I couldn't be anyone but me. I wasn't an actress. I was just Ellie.

Ellie Vanderwick.

The name echoed in my head. I was a Vanderwick. My scalp tingled, and tiny specks appeared all around me.

Specks of magic.

The first shadow figure was only steps from me.

"Harriet?" A man's voice said.

I nodded but didn't look up.

I could see the second set of feet coming up behind the first. Harriet was going to bind him.

"Do you have information about my mother?"

"Ellie?" The shadow said before turning and plunging the knife into Harriet's chest.

I gasped and jumped to my feet. The specks of magic had dissipated—I wouldn't know what to do with them in this situation anyway—but I didn't need magic to protect my family.

I launched myself onto the man's back and started hitting him over the head. He'd already attacked Harriet. I was next. Unless I did something about it.

"Get off me," the voice said. "Ellie, it's me."

Whoever this person thought they were, I didn't know them.

"You killed her," I screamed. "You killed Trinity. And now you want to kill us to cover up your mistake."

"I didn't make a mistake," the man said.

Then I caught a whiff of something—sandalwood and espresso beans.

I looked around. Xander had to be close if I could smell him.

"Ellie, it's me, Xander."

His voice was so close. How was he—oh!

I let go and slid to the ground.

"You killed Harriet?" I asked.

Xander looked at me like I was insane.

"I didn't kill anyone," he said. "I was protecting you."

"Then who is that?" I asked, pointing to the figure dressed in head-to-toe black on the ground.

"It's the person Harriet was trying to meet," Xander said. "The person she thought she wanted to kill."

We approached, and I noticed Xander hadn't actually stabbed the person. The knife was on the ground, and there was no blood.

"What did you do to them?" I asked.

"I kept them from killing you," he said.

"Right," I said. "But how?"

"Magic," Xander said.

"You did it," Harriet said, coming up behind us.

"Did what?" Xander said.

"You killed our cousin," she said. "Now we don't have to worry about him any—"

She stopped talking when Xander removed the unconscious person's mask.

"Who is she?" Harriet said. "This isn't our cousin."

"I know it's not," Xander said. "I can't believe you thought he'd meet you in what was obviously a trap." Xander sighed. "She's probably someone who works for him. Someone disposable."

A shiver ran down my spine. She didn't only work for our cousin. She worked for someone else too. "I know who she is."

"Who?" Harriet asked.

"She's Delilah's assistant," I said. "Her name is Linda."

"What would someone working for our cousin be doing as Delilah's assistant?" Harriet asked.

"Trying to get closer to you," Xander said. "And succeeding."

I could feel sparks flying through my hair. "Do you think she had something to do with Trinity's death?"

"I would guess she had everything to do with it," Xander said. "Check out her boots."

I glanced down to see stars on the soles of her boots. They were her footprints outside the theater that night.

"But now we can't ask her." I sighed.

"She's not dead," Xander said. "She'll wake up, eventually."

I glanced around the park. "Do you think he's somewhere watching?"

"He's not here," Xander said. "I don't think he ever was."

"What do you mean he never was?" Harriet asked.

"I've done some digging and found the man who seems to be your cousin has never stepped foot in Cliff Haven." Xander looked at Harriet. "He can't because of the protections Esme set up."

"But then why can I?" Harriet asked.

"Because you had good intentions," Xander said. "At least when it came to Ellie."

"So you're saying I've been wasting my time here?" Harriet narrowed her eyes at him.

Xander didn't reply.

"I mean, at least we got to meet," I said.

But Harriet didn't reply. She didn't even look at me. "You know," she said to Xander. "We had it under control. You think you know everything, but you probably scared him away."

"How are you any better than him if you're out here trying to kill him?" Xander asked.

"I'm trying to save my life and your little girlfriend's life."

Xander groaned.

If her words hadn't hurt enough, his obvious disgust when she referred to me as his girlfriend sent the pain to an excruciating level.

"Well," I said. "This has been fun, but I'm leaving now. Get her booked with Jake when she comes to."

Neither of them tried to stop me as I walked away.

I should have gone home. But I needed to tell Delilah what happened. Tell her that her assistant was responsible for her best friend's death.

Belinda was at the front desk when I walked into the B&B.

"Who died now?" Belinda asked.

"No one," I said. "Is Delilah here? I need to talk to her."

"She should be up in her room."

Belinda gave me her room number, and I headed up the stairs.

Delilah's room was right next door to the room Trinity had been staying in with Dylan.

It must have been so hard to live in Trinity's shadow all those years.

I knocked on the door and heard a grumble behind it. "I thought I told you to leave me alone for the rest of the night."

She tore the door open so hard I thought it might come off the hinges.

"Oh," she said. "What do you want?"

"I thought I'd tell you we found the person who killed Trinity."

Her face paled, and her eyes widened. "Who?"

"Can I come in?"

She nodded.

"You might want to sit down," I said.

The room was trashed. Clothes and shoes were everywhere—most of them still with tags and hanging halfway out of their respective shopping bags. Gucci, Langlin, Palmerson. So many brand names. She had to have spent thousands of dollars on these items.

"Sorry," she said. "Let me clear a place." She brushed a handful of clothes and other items off one of the wing-backed chairs so I could sit while she sat on the bed.

When we were both seated, she said, "So? Who was it?"

"I have reason to believe Linda, your assistant, was responsible for Trinity's murder."

Delilah's jaw dropped. "No," she said. "That can't be right."

"I haven't figured out the timeline of events yet, but I believe she used your friend's death as a warning to someone else."

Tears welled in Delilah's eyes. "But—I—"

"Do you have anything with Linda's handwriting on it?" I asked.

Delilah swiped the tears from her eyes and looked around. She hopped off the bed and dug through one of the shopping bags to pull out a receipt. "Here, that's her signature."

I glanced down at it. I couldn't be sure, but it looked like it might have been the same handwriting as was on the threatening note. Jake could probably have a handwriting analysis done or something.

"Can I keep this?" I asked.

She nodded. "But I don't understand. How could this have happened?"

"We're still piecing it all together," I said. "But I wanted you to have some closure. I know how much it was eating at you that Trinity had died."

"Where is Linda now?"

"She's on her way to jail," I said.

"Which means Melody will be out," Delilah said, her head drooping. "Which means I'll be out."

My heart ached for her. I didn't know what to say.

"But wait," her head shot back up. "What about Dylan's car? Do you think Linda did that too?"

I hadn't considered how she'd fit in with Dylan's death.

"Maybe," I said.

"I bet they were sleeping together. He seemed to be sleeping with basically everyone," Delilah said, blushing. "Or Melody really was responsible for that one."

I hated how much hope she placed on those last words. But I could understand why she'd feel that way.

"When she wakes up, I'm sure she'll tell the police everything."

hen I pulled into the driveway, I hesitated before driving Mona into the garage. "She's gone, isn't she?"

I could have sworn I felt Mona's wheel warm beneath my touch.

Penelope didn't greet me at the door when I walked in. She picked her head up from where she was lying at the bottom of the stairs and gave a tiny oink.

"I know," I said. "It's okay." But the tears winding tiny streams down my face told me it wasn't. Regardless of how guarded she was, she was still my family. The only family I had. "I'll miss her too."

I dropped my satchel on the kitchen island and then walked upstairs.

Penelope snuggled up in her little bed, and I cozied up in mine. I hadn't even glanced in Dewdrop. Part of me wanted to still believe Harriet was there. That she'd be pouring over her clues at the dining room table the following day.

But if our cousin wasn't in Cliff Haven, then there was no reason for Harriet to be either. Not even a reason as good as family. Harriet didn't know how much she took family for granted. Had no idea what it felt like to not have a single blood relative your entire life.

I didn't sleep. I kept playing everything over and over in my head. Harriet. Xander. Linda.

When it became too much to take, I tiptoed upstairs to the attic and opened the journal.

I had every intention of simply writing down what I was thinking, but instead, it opened to a page I'd never been able to read until now.

I can't believe I'm pregnant. I always thought I'd have a child—a daughter—but not for a few more years at least. And not with a man I can hardly stomach. Thankfully, he's gone. For good. He'll never step foot in this town again. And he'll never get the chance to have a son. He doesn't deserve a son when he can't appreciate the daughters he has.

I hear Veronique named her little girl Ambeline. Of course, she hates me now that she knows I too will have a child by him. But I can only hope that someday our daughters will be friends, if not like the sisters they are.

I read the words four or five times over. Maybe when everything was settled with our other cousin, Harriet would come back.

When I woke up the next morning, I made coffee, pulled my phone out of my satchel, and plugged it in. While I waited for it to charge enough to turn on, I grabbed the receipt Delilah had given me.

I looked it over more closely. The more I looked at it, the more I realized the signature looked nothing like the handwriting on the threatening note. The receipt was from a store in Des Moines. I glanced at the calendar pinned to my wall. The date of the purchase was the same as when Delilah had claimed to be shopping.

I glanced back at the calendar. Was that the right date? I thought back to make sure.

But if that was Linda's handwriting, then she would have been the one in town shopping. Meaning she couldn't have been the one to kill Trinity.

My heart dropped. Delilah had to have done it. The receipts she'd handed Jake hadn't had any signatures on them that I could remember.

Or she could have forgotten her story about shopping that day. Heck, she probably didn't even know what Linda bought on which days.

I had to call Jake, but my phone wasn't working. It had been charging long enough to turn on. But it wouldn't.

"I didn't do it, you know," a voice said behind me.

I whipped around to find Linda standing in the doorway.

"How did you—"

"You should really lock your doors."

I left them unlocked in hopes Harriet might return overnight.

"I know you didn't kill Trinity," I said.

"Or Dylan, though I wouldn't have minded that one." She shrugged. "He was a jerk."

"Why are you here?"

"I was looking for Harriet," she said. "I suspect she's not here any longer. She truly has a one-track mind. I bet she had you convinced she cared about you—about your mom?"

I shifted from one foot to the other. "What do you know about my mother?"

Her cheeks rose as she grinned. "More than you, obviously. And much more than your silly little cousin. She thinks she's doing the right thing—going after my employer—but she's missing the whole picture."

"And what picture is that?" I needed to keep her talking, especially if she knew something about my mom.

"Wouldn't you like to know?" She laughed. "I suppose all you thought you'd catch him, put him in jail, and you'd both live happily ever after?"

Had I thought that? Maybe. But when she said it, it sounded so stupid. So childish.

"Too bad she never cared about you in the first place. She was only using you to get to him."

Her words cut. The sweet Linda I'd felt bad for in the theater had been replaced with evil witch Linda.

"We may never know," I said, trying to keep my emotions off my face even though I was certain my hair was changing all sorts of colors. "I guess you made the trip out here for nothing."

She smiled. "Or did I?"

My scalp burned the way it did when I was in danger. "Harriet isn't here, and I already knew you didn't kill anyone."

"Not anyone in Cliff Haven."

I thought about the knives in the drawer on the other side of the island. There was no way I could get to those without her getting me with whatever magic she had first.

"Tell me," she said. "How did you figure out that my wannabe boss was responsible for her best friend's murder?"

"The receipt," I said, pointing to the countertop. "If you were shopping, you couldn't have been killing. And even though you had the boots with the stars, I'd venture to guess Delilah had a pair too."

"Oh, those were my boot prints," she said. "But the receipt isn't real."

I glanced over at it. "What do you mean it isn't real?"

"I mean, it's real," she said. "But the signature isn't. It's a fake."

"So you were there?" I was second-guessing everything I thought I knew. If she was there, she could have been the one who opened the trapdoor.

When she looked down at the threshold, I took a small step toward the back of the island. I had to get something to defend myself with.

"I was at the theater along with Trinity and Harriet and Delilah." She tried to take a step forward, but her leg was met with an invisible barrier.

The house's protections.

"I had a meeting there," she continued. "Plus, I

wanted to make sure Harriet got the message. I just didn't expect Delilah to be the one to do it."

"Who beat Trinity up before she fell?" I asked.

"Delilah," Linda said. "That's why the dressing room was trashed." Linda tried to reach a hand in but failed again. "In her defense, I don't think she meant to kill either of them. She was just full of anger."

"What do you mean? Either?"

"She cut the brake lines and had me plant the stuff in Melody's car." She shrugged. "I *was* her assistant," she said in her fearful voice again. "I had to do what she told me to."

"Even so," I said. "You won't get away with this. You're both going to jail."

"We'll see about that." The energy around us changed. She was trying to use her magic to get in.

Thankfully, it wasn't working.

I heard a squeal come from upstairs and then what sounded like a ball bouncing down the stairs.

"Penelope," I said, but before I could move, Penelope was charging at the door, squealing all the way.

Now, most people would laugh at the sight of a tiny pig running toward them, but Linda stopped whatever magic she was doing and held her hands out in front of her as if she was actually afraid of Penelope. "Stop," she said. "I'll go."

But Penelope didn't care. She charged right through the door and started biting Linda everywhere she could reach.

This gave me the opportunity to grab my phone—which was now working again—to call the police.

Linda turned to run, but Penelope was as fast as she was.

"Nine-one-one, what's your location?" The woman on the phone asked.

I gave her my address. "I need you to send someone fast. There's a murderer on my property."

"Again?" she asked. "Sorry." She paused. "I meant to say they'll be there shortly."

When the police pulled into the driveway, Linda was lying in the snow in the fetal position while Penelope stood guard. Blood trickled from various wounds on Linda's legs and arms.

I might have felt bad if she hadn't started it.

"She tried to attack me," I said as Deb got out of the car. "She's also an accessory to murder. Or assistant to murder. Or whatever you call someone who helps someone else murder people."

"If she's the assistant," Deb said, "who's the actual murderer."

34

Many of the cast members were already in the dressing room getting ready when I walked in with Deb and Jake behind me.

One of those cast members was Delilah.

"Did you find her?" Delilah asked, spinning around in her chair.

"We did," I said. "And she's confessed to everything."

Delilah nodded but looked slightly confused. "That's great."

"Which means," Melody said, appearing in the doorway, "I get my role back."

Katie stood and rushed to her daughter, wrapping Melody in a huge hug. "I knew you didn't do it."

"Uh, no," Delilah said. "The role is mine now. I did the dress rehearsal."

"Yes, but you also committed murder," I said.

She whipped around toward me. "What do you mean? Linda confessed."

"Linda confessed to her part in the crimes," I said. "But she also threw you under the metaphorical bus."

Delilah glared at me. "She's lying."

"If only she was," I said. "I guess we could go back to the cameras at the stores you supposedly shopped at the night of Trinity's murder. They'd tell us you were never there. Or we could go through your room and find the orange wig you wore the night you pulled the lever. And the Langlin boots." I'd only remembered seeing the bag in Delilah's room with the brand name Langlin on it after Jake had taken Linda into custody. I was willing to bet the pair of boots with the stars were buried somewhere in Delilah's B&B room. "But what sealed the deal were these." I held up the notes Delilah had written during rehearsals when she was observing Melody. "See that loop over the i?" I pointed to it. "It's the same one as on the threatening note you left for Trinity."

Delilah's eyes widened.

"You told us you hadn't been in town," I continued, "but you were at the café the day before. We all thought it was Trinity because you had the same wig, but I should have known it was you when you ordered the same meal just yesterday."

"Don't forget the part about her father," Deb said.

"Right," I said. "Your father owns a car lot, right? And you worked in his shop for years growing up. I'd venture to guess you knew how to use the side cutters to cut those brake lines."

Delilah stood in silence, her face getting redder and redder until she finally said. "I didn't mean for Trinity to die."

"Really?" I asked. "Is that why you beat the snot out of her before pulling the lever? You must have hated her to want to hurt her that badly."

"I'm as good an actress as she was," Delilah said. "But I didn't want her to die."

"And I bet it made you furious when you saw Melody with Dylan at the café right after he was with you," I said.

Delilah crossed her arms over her chest. "I think I need a lawyer."

"That's a good idea," Jake said before reading her her rights and cuffing her.

As Deb was leading Delilah out the door, Delilah said to Melody, "It's too bad the dress was altered. It's going to be way too big on your perfect little frame."

"About that," Fran said. "I never got around to altering it. I guess I assumed we'd have Melody back."

Delilah looked like her face might explode at any moment.

"Good job," Jake said to me. "As always."

"Thanks," I said. "But I think you need to tell Xander about Linda." I leaned closer to him. "She's on the magical side."

"Why don't we tell him together?" Jake pointed to the door where Xander stood smiling.

Jake and I walked to Xander. While Jake filled him in and they made plans to get Linda extradited to a magical holding facility, I watched the cast gather around Melody with joy. It was the perfect ending. Except, I still had to say my line. And because the snow had let up and the roads had been plowed, the theater would be packed.

I sucked in a breath.

"I'm going to take off," Jake said.

"Are you coming to the show?" I asked.

"I wouldn't miss it for the world." He smiled and walked through the doors, leaving Xander and me staring at each other in an awkward silence.

"I'm really sorry about last night," Xander said. "One of us should have gone after you." He paused. "I should have gone after you. That's what friends do, right?"

The tingle in my scalp told me my hair was changing. "But you didn't."

"I had to talk to Harriet. Then Linda got away, and we couldn't find her," he said. "But that makes no difference. I should have been there for you last night, and I should have been there for you this morning. I'm just glad Penelope knew what to do."

"The house did too," I said. "I don't think anything was going to hurt me."

He nodded. "Do you forgive me?"

I smiled. "Of course, I do."

"Good," he said, then turned to look at the other cast members. "They seem happy to have Melody back."

"She's an essential part of this play," I said. "And they're all practically family." I glanced down at my feet. "Why did she leave?"

Xander didn't say anything for a minute, then he put his hands on my shoulders, sending zaps of electricity down my body. "She's so focused on her mother's death she couldn't see the good thing she had in front of her."

"She's my only family," I said. "And now she's gone too."

"She may be your only blood relative," Xander said.

"But look around. These people are your family."

I looked up and around at the smiling faces.

"Katie, Nancy, Fran, Amy, Bonnie, Bex, Jake," he said. "I could keep going."

My heart felt like it was growing in size. He was right. I had a family right here. They might not be blood relatives, but they treated me as one of their own.

"And me," Xander said, hooking a finger under my chin and moving my gaze back to his. "I'm your friend, which means I'm your family too."

I wanted him to kiss me so badly it hurt. If I moved onto my tiptoes, our lips would touch. But he'd said friends. And I needed to respect his boundaries.

"Thank you," I finally said. He brought his lips down and kissed me on the forehead. "Now get out there and say that line."

***

Nancy and Hank opened the play as Santa and Mrs. Claus. All the children oohed and ahhed.

When Melody rose from beneath the stage through the trapdoor—almost as if she was resurrecting it from its cursed past—the entire crowd cheered.

The play was perfect. Not a single person missed a cue or forgot their lines.

And as the play was coming to an end, I could feel the rest of the cast on pins and needles.

My line was coming up. This time I would say it because this time it meant something. I wouldn't be acting. I would be telling my truth.

I looked into the crowd to see Jake and Xander, Nancy and Hank, Fran and Amy, and everyone else watching with smiles on their faces.

Melody finished her monologue and turned to go off stage.

I searched for the glimmers, but I didn't need magic.

With a voice loud and clear, I said, "And looking around at all our family, we finally knew we were home."

***

Thank you so much for reading *Spotlight Scandal*!

Don't miss the next book in the Magical Mane Mystery series—*Tango Trouble* releasing July 6th!

I would be honored and eternally grateful if you would post a review on Amazon and/or Goodreads about the book.

Also, I love hearing from readers! Email me at stellabixbyauthor@gmail.com.

XOXO,

Stella Bixby

ACKNOWLEDGMENTS

This book was a struggle and so many people helped pull me through it.

My family—thank you so much for putting up with my constant whining and grumbling.

Shawna—thank you for always being there to lend an ear and give wise advice.

The Brooklyn Book Club—I love being in your presence. You guys are awesome!

My beta readers—your advice and feedback is crucial to my process. Thank you one hundred times over.

My ARC readers—thank you for reading my books and sending me sweet messages. You are so amazing.

My readers—your kind words keep me going. Thank you so much for reading my books.

God—I cannot thank You enough for blessing me with the life I have. I realize how lucky I am to be able to write and be with my family every single day.

ABOUT THE AUTHOR

Stella Bixby is a native Coloradan who loves to snow-board, pluck at the guitar, and play board games with her family. She was once a volunteer firefighter and a park ranger, but now spends most of her time making up stories and trying to figure out what to cook for dinner.

Connect with Stella on Facebook, Twitter, and Instagram @StellaBixby.

Stella loves to hear from her readers!
www.stellabixby.com